MW00779908

COILHUNTER

BOOKS BY DEAN F. WILSON

THE CHILDREN OF TELM

The Call of Agon
The Road to Rebirth
The Chains of War

THE GREAT IRON WAR

Hopebreaker
Lifemaker
Skyshaker
Landquaker
Worldwaker
Hometaker

THE COILHUNTER CHRONICLES

Coilhunter
Rustkiller

HIBERNIAN HOLLOWS

Hibernian Blood
Hibernian Charm

A COILHUNTER CHRONICLES NOVEL

COILHUNTER

DEAN F. WILSON

Cover illustration by Duy Phan

First Edition 2017

ISBN 978-1-909356-18-4

DIOSCURI PRESS

Published by Dioscuri Press
Dublin, Ireland

www.dioscuripress.com
enquiries@dioscuripress.com

Welcome to the Wild North

CONTENTS

Chapter

Chapter One

RUM-HOLE

H is boots made a rhythmic thud against the floor, drawing the attention of everyone in the room. His boots were the first thing you noticed. Then the eyes travelled up, saw the long, deep blue coat and the holstered pistols, and turned away swiftly again when they spotted the mask and tubes beneath that deep blue hat.

Thud.

The people who recognised him had a dozen different names for him, and all of them were grim. The Coilhunter. The Sandsweeper. The Masked Menace. The people who didn't recognise him would come up with new names of their own very soon.

Thud.

He kept an even pace, slow and steady, the kind of pace that was at odds with the frantic heartbeats of the onlookers at the inn. One of his arms swung like a pendulum, and it reminded people of the fleeting pace of time. The other arm did not move at all; it stayed at his side, close to his gun.

Thud.

A little mechanical duck waddled along behind him, creaking and squeaking, its wide eyes matching those of the people who dared to look. It was a toy, a kind of wind-up device full of springs and cogs, and yet many knew that it was a dangerous toy.

Thud.

He scoured the room with his eyes, piercing everyone, almost piercing the walls as well. The mask accentuated his stare, as did the black lines around his eyes. The brim of his hat cast a shadow that made the whites of his eyes stand out even more.

The final *thud* seemed a little louder. He halted, then reached for his coat pocket, and people flinched. He held up a rolled-up poster, and let it unfurl noisily in his hand, revealing the mugshot of a criminal, *Old Mad Jack*, the ominous word *Wanted*, and the prize of one hundred coils beneath. Cold, hard coils, traded for the cold, hard dead.

"This man," he said, his voice muffled by the mask, yet not muffled enough to hide the grit. "Ya seen 'im?" He prodded the paper with his dust-covered finger, the kind of finger exposed almost constantly to the sand and the sun. The kind of finger that spent a lot of time on a trigger.

Most heads turned away. A few braver souls gave the slightest shake of their heads. There was no one brave enough to talk. The duck shuffled up to the Coilhunter's foot and gave an ominous little quack.

A puff of dark smoke came from a vent on the left side of the Coilhunter's mask. No one knew why. On the other side, pipes connected the mask to a cylinder on his back, where he also kept a strapped guitar and a four-barrel shotgun.

"Ya see," he croaked, "I know this man came this

way, and there ain't no other rum-hole for miles. They say Old Mad Jack's a drinker, and I say a drinker cannot pass a rum-hole without poppin' in for a drink."

The barmaid tensed up at the bar, polishing a dirty glass a little more vigorously than before.

"So," the Coilhunter continued, "let me repeat this, and let me tell ya that I don't like repeatin' things: this man … any o' you here fine fellows seen 'im?"

Three men playing cards in the corner exchanged nervous glances. The Coilhunter caught them, and strolled over. The duck stayed where it was in the centre of the room, watching everyone.

"You boys," the Coilhunter said, gesturing with the chin of his mask to them. "Good game, is it?"

"J-j-just a game o' Don," the oldest replied, the cards trembling in his hands.

"You wan' in?" the youngest asked. The others scolded him with their eyes.

The Coilhunter drew real close, close enough that they could see the cracks in his weathered skin. "I want an answer to my question." He hammered the poster onto the table, over the cards. Old Mad Jack stared up at them. "Get a real good look-see, and each o' ya tell me one by one that you ain't seen him 'fore I put his ugly mug down on this table."

The youngest looked like he was about to say something. Only the stares of his companions stopped him. The Coilhunter placed a hand on his shoulder and turned his chair around. The youth held up his cards before him like a shield.

"You look like a smart boy," the Coilhunter said. "The kind o' boy with a good memory and a good eye.

Maybe a good eye for faces. Maybe a good mouth for speakin' who those faces are."

"I might have—" He cut himself short, silenced by the glances of the others.

"Where's your manners, boy? You're talkin' to me. You *look* at me." He gestured with his hand towards his own grim eyes. The exhaust in his mask let out another menacing puff of smoke.

The young man looked back, keeping his cards up. They wouldn't help him.

"I ain't got all day," the Coilhunter told him. "You ain't got all day either."

"H-h-he's out b-back."

The Coilhunter smiled. He knew they could not see it behind his mask, but they could see it in his eyes.

"He ain't out back," a voice said from far across the room behind him. As the Coilhunter turned, he saw Old Mad Jack standing behind the bar, rifle in hand. "He's right here."

Chapter Two

OLD MAD JACK

Old Mad Jack fired, and the Coilhunter threw himself to the floor, his guitar giving a twang to follow the overture of the gunfire. The bullet tore through the table of the cardplayers, and all three men leapt up with the splinters, casting their cards—even the ones up their sleeves—into the air.

The Coilhunter was ready for the second shot, his own right pistol in hand. The barflies scattered at the sight, and Old Mad Jack was already halfway on the trigger. Both guns fired in almost perfect unison, but Jack wasn't just old and mad—he was quick. He dived behind the bar, pulling the barmaid down with him. The Coilhunter knew he didn't do that for chivalry, and he knew Old Mad Jack would show why he did it soon enough.

The two bullets whizzed by each other, Jack's punching a hole in the wall, the Coilhunter's smashing through a row of bottles behind the bar. The beer and wine cascaded down with the shards. *What a waste.* The Coilhunter never thought that about blood.

The other people in the saloon bolted for the door. It was get out now while everyone was in their trenches, or get stuck between them in the no man's land. The Coilhunter was glad they left. There were no *Wanted* posters for them, and if they wound up dead, he'd feel it only just that he pose for one of his own.

The Coilhunter stood up slowly, letting the dust of the gunpowder pour down his coat. Some of it stuck, mingling with the sand of the desert. He pointed his gun towards the bar. He could have taken the other one from its holster, or the one on his back, or the one up his sleeve. He didn't bother. He only needed one to do the job. The other hand could haul the body outside.

"I've got young Billie here," Jack shouted.

The Coilhunter couldn't see, but he heard the barmaid's muted whimpers.

"You let me go free now, and I let her go free, y'hear?"

"I hear ya," the Coilhunter said. He heard him all right. He just didn't agree.

"I wanna hear you promise that, cross yer heart an' all that."

The Coilhunter cocked his gun. "Hope to die?"

"Don't you go mockin' me with words or I'll make a mockery o' you with this here sweet lass' brains. I know you, Nox, and I know what'll haunt yer dreams. It'll be your downfall one of these days, mark my words, it will."

"And what will be yours, *Jack*?"

A finger rose above the bar. The Coilhunter could have cleaved it off with a bullet, but he waited. "That's up to him above," Jack said. "But it won't be here, I swears ya."

The Coilhunter made a slight adjustment to his mask; the straps on the back bore into the sunburnt marks of his neck. "Then why don't we go outside, and you can keep your promise, and I can keep mine."

"You go out one way, and I go out the other, and poor Billie here doesn't come to no harm."

"You say you know me, so then you know I can't let you go."

"But you know *me*, Nox," Jack replied.

He did, and that was what worried him. Poor Billie was barely eighteen. She looked like she hadn't been long behind the bar. It looked like she wouldn't be long behind it in the future either.

"If I let you go," the Coilhunter said, "you'll go on to rape and kill elsewhere."

"What's it to ya?"

"Well, I can't allow that."

"You go around playin' sheriff," Jack said, "but you ain't no sheriff. The Wild North's got no lawmakers an' no lawkeepers. That suits us all just fine. Leave it to him above, Nox. Give it up, 'fore you give up the ghost and have to face him."

"I'll face him with head high," Nox said. "Will you?"

Jack did not reply. Maybe he thought about his crimes. All those rapes. All those murders. All those women. He didn't kill men if he didn't have to. Only women, because he wanted to. A hundred coils wasn't enough for someone like him. Nox didn't do it for the money. Justice was payment enough.

"This'll be ugly," Jack said, shifting behind the bar.

The Coilhunter could hear Billie's whimpers

escalate. He could only imagine that Jack had just pressed a gun against her head. It suggested he had swapped his rifle for a pistol. That'd make him faster. Old Mad Fast Jack. He kept getting adjectives added to his name.

"It's always ugly," the Coilhunter replied.

"I'm gonna come out now," Jack said, "and you're gonna put your pistol away."

Old Mad Fast Psychic Jack.

The Coilhunter didn't reply.

Jack rose slowly, hauling Billie before him as if that mattered. She wasn't big enough to shield all of him. It was the pistol to her temple that mattered more. His other hand was wrapped around her mouth to stop her from screaming. Funny that. He didn't mind them screaming before.

Nox slowly lowered his weapon.

"You put that there back in its box." Jack urged him with his eyes.

The Coilhunter holstered the pistol, and he did it real slow, slow enough to let him hook a little canister from his belt onto his little finger, and slow enough to hide it in his hand.

"None of yer tricks now, y'hear?" Jack warned, burrowing the barrel of his pistol into poor Billie's head, eliciting a louder, yet still muffled, cry from her. Her eyes were wide with terror. The kind of terror of the young who hadn't seen enough of the Wild North. Jack's eyes had no terror. They didn't even have hate. They were empty. If the eyes were the window to the soul, then that emptiness wasn't at all surprising. The soul didn't last long here. The Wild North killed it in everyone, sooner or later. Sooner for most.

Again the Coilhunter didn't reply. That way, he didn't have to lie.

Jack shuffled out slowly from behind the bar, dragging poor Billie with him, over the broken glass and spilt gunpowder, over the splinters and cards. He was out in the open now, and the Coilhunter could see a lot of places he could have landed a bullet. Too bad Jack was quick. He'd have one in Billie's head too.

"I see you brought yer pet," Jack said, nodding towards the little mechanical duck, standing as still as the Coilhunter in the centre of the room. There was no terror or hate or soul in its eyes, those painted on eyes. It did what it was told. To it, the Coilhunter was God. "You're a fruit, y'know that?" Jack continued. "I've met eccentric bounty hunters in my time, but you're somethin' else."

"Yes," Nox said. "I'm the law."

Jack stepped out further, pushing Billie in front of him. "Not today you ain't."

The Coilhunter eyed him coldly. He knew what Jack would see in his eyes. There was hate there. And there even was a soul. But it was covered in a shell of loathing. Maybe that was the only way he got to keep it.

Jack sidled towards the door.

"You leave her behind when you get out," the Coilhunter told him.

Jack smiled at him, revealing his blackened teeth.

The Coilhunter turned with him, his hands raised, yet half-clenched, hiding the little round capsule beneath his fingers.

Jack backed out of the swinging doors, pulling poor Billie through with him. How many times had he done that with a young woman? How many people had watched on?

As Billie's feet disappeared through the doors, the Coilhunter cast the orb across the floor behind her. It rolled through just as the doors swung shut. He walked to the nearest window and peered outside. Jack was still backing away slowly, waiting for the Coilhunter to follow, waiting for the gun. The gun wouldn't come just yet.

The little orb rolled up to Jack's foot and stopped. He looked down, confused, and his confusion grew when it cracked open, and out came half a dozen little butterflies. Mechanical butterflies.

The Coilhunter suddenly launched himself through the window, aiming a grappling gun at Billie. He fired, while Jack was still distracted, and the hook took a hold of a strap on her dungarees. He pulled hard. She stumbled forward, out of Jack's arms, and out of the line the bullet made as it left Jack's pistol.

The butterflies flapped around the criminal. He swatted them as they came near his face, knocking one of them into the sand. Then they started to release a green gas, and he shook his head as the fumes made him weak. He turned away, half-running, half-staggering, making for the large black monowheel parked nearby. The mechanical insects pursued him, landing on him, digging their little claws into his face, and releasing more of the gas in their tiny bodies, until he fell face-first into the dirt, one hand reaching out for the vehicle.

Two of the butterflies came for Billie and the Coilhunter, releasing the same noxious gas, which made Billie faint. It did nothing for the Coilhunter, and he eventually crushed them both between his hand.

"Sorry, girl," he said to Billie, as he let her down gently to the ground. "It'll wear off."

He walked slowly over to Old Mad Dirt-faced Jack and kicked him onto his back. His smug smile wasn't there any more. His eyes were closed, so you didn't have to see the emptiness. Not that it really mattered. The Coilhunter had stared many straight in the eye.

Nox took out his pistol with his right hand and made an X with the index and middle fingers of his left over his chest.

"Cross my heart," he said, before pulling the trigger.

Chapter Three

ONE WHEEL AND TWO BODIES

"You, boy," the Coilhunter said, pointing to a child of about five years, playing nearby with marbles in the cracks of the earth. The child looked up, surprised. He'd been staring at the bodies, letting his marbles drop one by one from his hands.

"See this woman," the Coilhunter continued. The boy looked at Billie and gave a dumb nod. "You find someone to look after her." The boy continued to stare at him until Nox flicked a coil his way, which dislodged one of the marbles from the dirt. The child took it up with both hands. A whole coil. He probably hadn't seen one in his life. He stared at the iron currency, a flattened coil stamped with the face of the Iron Emperor. That sense of wonder was precious. Pity it wouldn't last.

"Boy," the Coilhunter said. The child hopped up, dashing away a bit, then halting and looking back, unsure if he should take his marbles too. He caught the glare of the Coilhunter and decided to leave them. Nox spotted three other boys nearby, lounging against the side of a building, watching those abandoned marbles like vultures. One thing the Coilhunter knew for sure: they wouldn't take them while he was there.

20

He tipped his hat to poor, unconscious Billie. Unconscious was better than dead. He turned to Old Mad Dead Jack, who was painting the ground a shade of scarlet. There never was enough colour in the Wild North. Nox just thought it was a pity the most vibrant one was red.

He hauled the body up and pulled it closer to the monowheel. That wasn't Jack's getaway vehicle. It belonged to the Coilhunter. It was a large ring, which you sat inside, on top of the engine, clutching a small steering wheel. In a fairer climate he might have had a thin tyre around the outside of the wheel, but in the sinking sands he needed the thicker treads of a landship instead. That wheel rotated around the inner structure, so when it rolled, you didn't roll with it. You could tilt and turn, and gravity kept you firmly in place. It was as black as the blackest night, which made it stand out strongly against the yellow sands. Nox liked it like that. He wanted the criminals to know he was coming for them.

The Coilhunter put Jack's body in a large box behind the seat, his arms and legs dangling over the sides. You didn't want to be in the passenger seat of that vehicle. It usually always meant you were dead.

He drove off, just as the boy returned with his father, who froze when he saw the Coilhunter. Nox tipped his hat to him, then revved the engine, sending a plume of grey smoke up behind him, like a veil. When it settled, he would be gone.

He rolled through the dunes, the landship treads leaving deep tracks in the sand. Sometimes the land conspired against him, and travel was difficult, but other times it worked with him, shifting the grains to cover his tracks. Maybe there were prayers to say. He'd seen a lot of people praying them. But the land seemed to change its mind all the time. If there were gods, you couldn't trust them. Better to forge your path alone. Hell, better to see if there was a bounty on those gods too.

The journey was long, and he was thankful that Jack was a recent kill. He hadn't started to smell yet, aside from his natural stench, and the whiff of alcohol. At least he hadn't soiled himself, like some did. And he hadn't started to decompose yet. That was the worst smell. With the unsympathetic eye of the sun glaring down on them, that wouldn't be long setting in.

Every day reinforced a realisation he once had: that the land was trying to kill you, and not just you—everyone. It conspired with everything. There was no escaping it. You could only delay it. Sooner or later, it'd get you. The tribespeople tried to work with it, tried to appease it, communing with the spirits of the sand. But Nox didn't see spirits there—he saw a devil in every grain.

He passed between two granite cliffs, which met together at one point far ahead, a curved bridge of rock that some dared to traverse. From it hung at least a dozen broken, bird-pecked bodies, a warning from and to the rival gangs. Every time he passed beneath them, and it was often, the Coilhunter was reminded of a phrase General Rommond of the Resistance once told him: *You hang your heroes. That way they'll never disappoint you.* It also brought to mind his own retort: *But what about your enemies? What about the villains? What do we do with those?*

Chapter Four

THE BOUNTY BOOTH

It wasn't hard to find bounties in the Wild North. The Wanted posters were pasted everywhere, on the side of buildings, at the back of bars, right beside the finest whiskey. Hell, even the wind helped out sometimes, pasting the odd poster onto the prickles of a cactus. Then again, if you were on the poster, that wasn't helping at all. Told you the land was trying to get you.

If you wanted to cash in, though, well, you had to go somewhere special. That was the Bounty Booth, right on the easternmost edge of the Wild North, bordering Regime-controlled territory. It was barely a building at all, more like a ramshackle shed sitting out all by its lonesome in the empty expanse of the desert. The wood leant inwards, old and creaking.

The Coilhunter pulled up, leaning the monowheel to one side and kicking out the support stand. Old Mad Dead Jack's arm lopped forward, reaching out to graze the desert floor. You can't blame him for wanting to touch solid earth again. That'd be his home soon enough.

Nox stomped through his own well-worn tracks up to the front door, which looked a little lopsided, letting the whistling breeze in through a large crack in the corner. Nox liked his music, but you never quite got used to the tunes the weather made. They were always haunting.

Nox halted as soon as he opened the door just an inch. The smell was different.

No tobacco, he thought. That wasn't like Waltman.

The Coilhunter sniffed again, just to be sure. The sniff was augmented by the mask he wore, making it sound a little mechanical, and a little frightening.

He stepped in, pushing the door wide, almost forcing it off its hinges. That wasn't hard. This old shack could've been huffed and puffed away. That sniff almost did it. The door clattered off a pile of crates behind, shuddering. The man inside, standing behind the desk, shuddered too.

Not Waltman, Nox thought. *Unless he got younger and prettier*. That wasn't possible. The dry heat cracked the skin as much as it cracked the earth. But you were lucky if you got to age at all. There were a lot of young and pretty souls in heaven.

"Who are you?" Nox rasped, keeping his hand close to his side, hovering, fingers craving the sudden, swift sling of a gun.

That man who wasn't Waltman, who didn't smoke, and who hadn't yet been touched by the dry fingers of the desert, stared back from beneath his straw hat and black curls. He was new around here. You could tell. He didn't duck for cover for a start.

"Hardwell," the man said. "Logan Har—"

"Where's Waltman?" the Coilhunter interrupted. He glanced around the room instinctively, looking

25

for the body. There was always a body. If there wasn't, maybe it'd be you.

"I don't know."

"See, that disappoints me. I prefer people who know things."

"Well, I know *things*, but—"

"You're new."

"Eh, yes, I am. Who're you?"

"That's how I know you're new."

"Ah."

"Comin' back to ya, eh?"

"Well, I was … warned about you. The Coilhunter, right?"

"If you're on the right side of the law, I'm just huntin' coils. If you're on the wrong side, well, I'll be huntin' you."

"I'm just a bounty operator."

"You're Waltman's replacement."

"I guess."

"And you don't know what happened to him."

"No."

"See, that'd worry me."

"Why?"

"Well, wouldn't you like to know?"

"Know what?"

"Who replaces you."

He knew that unnerved Hardwell, but that son of a gun never played ball. He might have had a young face, but right now it might as well have been granite.

"I've brought you somethin'," Nox said. He popped out, then hauled Old Mad Dead Jack inside, and let the body slump to the floor. That was the thing about the Bounty Booth. There was always a body.

"Ah," Hardwell said.

"Consider it a welcome gift. You know, first day on the job."

"Old Mad Jack?"

"He ain't gettin' any older now."

"I think he was one hundred coils." Hardwell rummaged through the piles of Wanted posters.

"I think you're right."

"Let me just see if—"

"Let me just help you out there," Nox said, pulling a rolled-up poster from his pocket. He tossed it to Hardwell, who fumbled with it until it struck the desk. He unfurled it to reveal Jack's ugly mug. It was a bit prettier than the one he had now though. And he wasn't smiling anymore.

"All seems to be in order," Hardwell said. He pulled open a drawer and took out a bag of coils. He threw it towards the Coilhunter, who caught it with those lightning fast reflexes.

Nox paused, clutching the bag. "I don't do it for the money, you know."

"I never said you did."

No, Nox thought, *but I can see you thinkin' it.* They all thought it. After all, he was a bounty hunter. He was the Coilhunter. He never gave himself that name, but it stuck. It stuck like the criminals stuck to the Wild North, like the flies stuck to dung.

"For me, it's about justice," Nox explained. He knew what Hardwell must be thinking: *Why are you explaining yourself?* He didn't need to, but he felt he should. Hell, he felt like his own kind of criminal for taking the money. But he needed that. There weren't enough of his type in these lands. He had to make up for it by being resourceful. You couldn't be that without resources.

"For us it's about justice too," Hardwell replied. He straightened up his Regime uniform, that black leather with the red cross and black square on the shoulder, the mark of that new governing force in the south and the east, and heading west. It didn't touch the north, not here. This was Coilhunter territory. Hardwell hadn't learned that yet, because he was new. He was an Iron Empire man, one of those so-called "demons" that came from another realm. He looked pretty human to Nox, but to him that was not much better at all.

Nox humphed. It was only justice for them if it aligned with their plans. They had posters up for all sorts, not just the criminals. They had one of General Rommond, leader of the Resistance, and one of Taberah Cotten, his right-hand gal. Sometimes Nox would pull those posters down, just in case the other bounty hunters got their sights on them. Other times he didn't bother. Those two were tough. They could take care of themselves.

"I suppose I'll see you again some time," Hardwell said. Seemed like he was trying to get rid of him. Nox couldn't help but think: *maybe like he got rid of Waltman too.*

"Sooner than you think," Nox replied, spotting a new poster on the wall. It was a woman. You got your fair share of those up there too. But this one had a familiar name. *Handcart Sally.* She was known for robbing the mines in the east. Iron mines. Those were precious to the Iron Empire, so it was no surprise that they were offering a big reward for her, bigger than Old Mad Jack. It said *Dead or Alive*, but once the Coilhunter got on the trail, it might as well have just read *Dead*.

He yanked the poster from the wall and rolled it up.

"Got another one already?" Hardwell inquired.

"Yeah. Well, I haven't got her yet."

He glanced at the line of faces as he left. There was old Rommond again, looking prim and proper, like he always did. And there was Taberah, looking fiery as ever. Yeah, they could take care of themselves. But this one, this Handcart Sally—well, the Coilhunter'd take care of her.

Chapter Five

THAT SAME DAMN JOURNEY

The sun was setting, which was a kind of mercy, but it wouldn't be long before it vanished altogether, letting the night take its place. You had to fend off the icy cold then, and whatever else came out of cracks in the earth.

Nox didn't know where to start with the search for Handcart Sally, but he usually went to the border towns first. There weren't many of those. Hell, there weren't many towns in the first place. There were dens all right, and hideaways, the kind of places the convicts holed up. But he needed a place to start, and people to ask. He had a special way of asking.

Yet this was Sunday evening, which meant it was getting close to a special day for the Coilhunter. Monday meant a lot to him, though not for the right reasons. No matter what he was doing, he dropped it all—contracts, bodies—to head far west, out of the no man's land of the Wild North and onto the dirt roads near Copperfort, one of the cities not yet taken by the Regime.

The night deepened, forcing him to turn on the headlights on the monowheel, powered by a big battery in the back. It was a faint light, and the battery wouldn't last for long, but in a world of steam and iron, this was a godsend. Pity there didn't seem to be any gods left to send more.

He bypassed Copperfort, where he knew he wasn't welcome, and carved a path through the unmarked roads of the desert. He'd carved those paths before, but the sands were always shifting. That was good for him, when he didn't want to be followed, but it was bad for him when he was following someone else. He had a good nose, and a great sense of direction, but he'd lost the trail before, when it really mattered. Regardless of where he was or what he was doing, he was always looking to find it again.

The journey was long, long enough that he had to bring an extra canister of diesel. You didn't want to get stuck out there, in day or night. He could already feel the monowheel getting sluggish, but he knew he wasn't far now. The air seemed to change when he got close. Maybe that was just the memories. Maybe it was something more.

He arrived at a small cemetery, untouched by grave-robbers, and largely untouched by the weather. The winds were less fierce here, the sun less oppressing, and the night air less piercing. Even the ground itself was better. This was near the farming lands, the few remaining patches of earth that got a little rain. It was why he brought them here. It kind of reminded him of how things used to be, before it all went bad, before it all crumbled apart.

He climbed off the monowheel and took something out of the box in the back, cradling it in his hands, keeping it away from the prying wind and the spying stars. There were a few out tonight. He always wondered if maybe, just maybe, that was them. It helped a bit, but not enough.

He walked into the graveyard, bordered with a little iron fence. His boots didn't thump down like they normally did. His stride was slow, and his footfalls were soft.

He knelt down before three graves, which got progressively smaller. They had little headstones, with little phrases on them that didn't seem to do them justice. *Emma, beloved.* That was on the biggest. And boy was she beloved. Not just by Nox. By everyone. You couldn't meet Emma and not fall in love with her. She was a farmer's daughter, tough and tender at the same time. She tilled the earth, and she tilled hearts too, helping some seeds of hope and love grow there. She made him a good man. Her death made him bad again.

He didn't have a rose to put there. Those were hard to come by now. Sometimes you had to hire a smuggler for them. But if he did have one, he knew that while laying it down upon the grave, he'd feel the thorns through his gloves.

He turned his attention to the second grave. *Ambrose, a light doused too soon.* She was a gentle girl, the kind that'd interrupt her mother's farming to pick up a little insect and bring it to safety. She was fascinated by learning, and was often found asleep with her books. She knew all the names for the birds, knew all the types of fish. Hell, she even had names for the different types of clouds. She used to say that she wanted to be a professor when she grew up. Nox sighed. She never got the chance.

He turned to the last grave, the smallest yet. *Aaron, dear wild wanderer*. He was a curious boy, keen to explore. He didn't care to learn the names of rocks, but he wanted to climb them, and look out over the vast reaches, and then hike out to those other places he spotted from the heights. This caused Nox and Emma all kinds of worry, as he'd often disappear for a day or two in his travels. That child was happy with his own company. Nox hoped that wherever he was wandering at the moment, he was happy now.

He uncupped his hands, revealing a miniature monowheel, made up of little pipes and bits of wood and metal. Aaron used to ask him for one just like his, so he could travel farther, see more places. He wanted to explore the world. Nox refused, fearing the child would get into mischief, or get lost somewhere, or never come back. None of that mattered now.

He gave a sigh, echoed by the wind. He laid the toy down upon the grave. Perhaps the ghosts would play with it.

It'd been three years since it happened, and it never got any better. Time was supposed to heal wounds, and maybe somewhere else it did. But in this world, Altadas, it just seemed to make things fester.

He made that journey every week, without stop. It used to be every day, when the pain was raw, before it scabbed over with vengeance, before he buried it with the dead. Every week was enough. Enough to remember them by. Enough to reignite the anger. Enough to then forget a little before he did it all over again.

Forgetting was like ointment. But for him it only dulled the pain. It was still there, beneath the surface, beneath the cracks and crags, waiting.

"I'll find him," he said. "I'll find who did this. I'll keep searchin'." He paused, taking a deep breath, letting it rattle out of the mask with a puff of grey smoke. "I'll keep huntin'."

Chapter Six

BAD FOR BUSINESS

The journey back to the Wild North was always quicker. Maybe it was because he was trying to get away from the pain. Maybe it was because he was keen to inflict some of his own. He thought of himself as a noble man, though perhaps his own kind of noble. It meant he couldn't just take it out on anyone. They had to be bad. Good for him that the Wild North was full of bad.

There was a small shanty town on the border, with one foot on either side. Some say "the best of both worlds," but if both worlds are bad, maybe you just end up with the worst of both. They called it Edgetown, and living there was like living on the edge. They got fierce sandstorms, and often had to lock themselves in their cellars. When they emerged, those rickety wooden buildings were even more broken and battered than before.

He asked a few of the locals about Handcart Sally, showing them the poster, but hiding the reward. None of them had heard of her, it seemed, or they just didn't want to hear. Often it was better that way, for them. It meant you didn't have to take a side. Taking sides was dangerous. Yet, not giving the Coilhunter the information he wanted was dangerous too.

He saw a pedlar of goods on the town corner, with a crowd gathered around him. He seemed to be showing off a device for harvesting water. No wonder there was interest. Even the land must've been interested. He looked like a conman though, and maybe Nox could have stopped him, but the Wild North was a magnet for conmen and criminals. He had to be picky who he went after first.

So sometimes the conmen got lucky. And other times, he picked you.

"Tell me somethin', traveller," he said, drawing up to the crowd. They parted like a wave.

Funny, that, he thought. *Seems I got more control of water than this here harvester.*

"I d-don't want any trouble," the pedlar said. He was well-dressed. With all that con work, he could afford to be. "I'm just m-m-minding my own business."

"You're mindin' everyone's business here. Hell, you're looking after their businesses real good. Quite a generous soul ya got there to mind so many purses. It must be terrible heavy. Back-breakin' even."

"I, uh—"

"He's making water!" one of the women cried jubilantly.

"A magician, eh?" the Coilhunter asked, turning back to the pedlar. "Ya ain't pullin' coins out behind people's ears. No. You're pullin' 'em straight outta their pockets."

"Why, I never!"

"I can do a trick or two. I can pull lead out from

between your eyes."

If the crowd hadn't already backed away by now, that would've done it. They kept going. A machine that made water wasn't worth it if you weren't alive to drink it.

"You scared them off!" the pedlar complained.

"I didn't mean for that," the Coilhunter replied. "I was only tryin' to scare you."

"Well, you've rattled me all right. I'll be off then." He started to pack up his things. Nox grabbed his hand, and he let the machinery drop.

"Haven't I seen you before?" Nox inquired.

The pedlar's eyes widened. "No."

"Well, you look like you've seen me."

"We've all *heard* of you."

"Good things, I hope."

"I guess we all have to dream. And we all to make a living. That's all I'm doing here."

"Selling hope to the hopeless."

"Better than selling the other kind, huh? Some people bring the Hope drug up here too, you know, and we don't see you going after *them*. Just the legitimate traders like me."

"Oh, I go after them all right. If you don't see it, well, that's because it happens in the shadows. Hell, you don't wanna see it. But you … Sam Silver, right? … Legitimate." The Coilhunter gave a hoarse, chesty laugh, ending with a cough. "Oh, I ain't had a good laugh like that in a *long* time."

"Can you let go of my arm now?" the pedlar asked. He didn't beg, like most. He'd encountered the Coilhunter before, no doubt, and got off with a warning. Some people didn't learn their lesson. Sometimes you had to teach them.

With a suddenness that caught Sam Silver off guard, Nox pulled him up and across the table, casting him into the sand with a wallop. Just as suddenly, he leapt at the man, pinning him to the ground.

"There," he said. "I ain't holdin' your arm now, and I ain't holdin' your hand. I'm here to teach ya now, but when I ain't, you better learn on your own. See, I've seen you around, robbin' people right before their faces. You're a brazen type, Sam. You don't work in the shadows. You ain't afraid o' the light. It seems you ain't afraid of the law either. So, what are you afraid of? Shall we find out?"

Sam squirmed, but just like the venomous snakes that sometimes ended up in the Coilhunter's grasp, he couldn't wiggle free. "Let me go!"

"What, so you can go to another town and rob 'em there too?"

"I won't. I swear! I promise!"

"See, I like those words, but I like 'em better when people mean 'em."

"I mean them! I swear, I do! I really do!"

The Coilhunter wafted his hand at the side of his face. "Music to my ears. And you know, I love music. Hell, I love it so much I'm gonna play you somethin'."

The pedlar was confused, unsure if he should scream or sit back and listen.

The Coilhunter clambered off him and sat down on the sand nearby. He pulled his metal-plated guitar from his back and played a few notes, his fingers working the strings as quickly as he worked the triggers of his guns.

"Now," he said, resting his arms on the reinforced guitar. "That's my tune. If you're off somewhere tryin' to sell somethin' ya shouldn't, and you hear this." He played it again, quick and sudden, and now it was intimidating. "Well, you better run, boy, because I'll be comin' for ya."

Before Sam Silver could react, Nox pressed a hidden button on the guitar, which opened a secret chamber. Out of this came a thick smoke, which spread around the Coilhunter until he vanished into it. When it faded, which took some time, it seemed that the Coilhunter had vanished altogether. Yet, from just beyond the edge of hearing, there was the sound of a familiar tune.

Chapter Seven

THE BURG

Edgetown was no dice. If Handcart Sally had been through there, she'd been through quick and quiet. No one was giving her up. The best the Coilhunter could get was a rumour that she was away from the mines to get one of those amulets the women were all talking about. Could stop you getting knocked up, or so they said. As far as Nox was concerned, there was only one way you could stop that, but then you didn't get to have so much fun.

There weren't many amulet smugglers around these parts. They mostly served Regime territory down south, where the so-called "demons" reigned. If you didn't want a monster for a child, you'd pay a pretty penny for one of those necklaces. And if you were caught smuggling them, well, you'd pay with your pretty head.

Nox went to the only place you'd really find amulet smugglers in the Wild North: the Burg. That was the largest town there, perched on a plateau almost bang smack in the centre of all those fields of yellow and red. It was a trader's paradise, if there was any such thing as paradise. You got to make a buck at least, so long as you didn't run foul of the Dust Barons, who kept a kind of trader's law running through the streets. You paid your dues, and you were good to go. If you didn't, well, good luck to you, and good luck to those hands of yours too.

The Coilhunter pulled up close to the city, but not too close, or he'd have to pay for parking. There was nothing the Dust Barons wouldn't get you to pay for. That was how they got the name, because they'd almost charge you for the dust of the desert itself. They were the poor cousins of the Treasury down south, but that didn't mean they weren't trying their damnedest to get rich.

The Burg was a bit of a monument, half natural, half man-made, but all of it corrupted by man. The plateau must've been a hundred feet high, and the city itself wasn't much higher. They tried building up, but the fierce winds kept knocking them low. You can build on nature, but you can't quite tame it.

Nox strolled on through the southernmost of the Burg's eight gates, flicking a quarter coil over to the tollman, who gave him back just the tilt of his hat. The Coilhunter kept on going, shoving his way through the crowd, his gunslinger gait drawing a few wide eyes. No matter who you were looking for, you always seemed to find a dozen more you could probably add to the list.

Nox hated this place. There were just too damned many people, all trying to carve out a living, just like the city itself was carved out of the rock. You couldn't hear yourself think with all the yelling. Half-price this, a sale on that. You didn't so much as buy things as have them shoved down your throat. Yet, for all the trade going on, you wouldn't find Sam Silver there. No, he'd be too cheap to pay the toll.

The Coilhunter didn't ask about Handcart Sally. He thought he'd get to her the long way around by asking for the amulet smugglers instead. It wasn't quite as dangerous to ask about them here compared to down south, but it still made people uneasy.

"I won't have anything to do with them," a clothier told him, while simultaneously nodding his head to one of the back alleys. "How abouts I do you a deal on a neckerchief though." He waved a bunch of them. "You could replace that mask."

The clothier reached towards the mask, but Nox swatted his hand away. "I could replace that arm."

The Coilhunter followed the trail of nods and gestures until he found a quieter part of the city, packed instead with shadows. There was a beggar there, with a sign that read *Can't Walk, Can Sing*, and a bowl, and not much else. You didn't get many of them in the Burg, because the Dust Barons put a tax on begging too.

Nox knelt down beside the man. "Making much business?"

"See for yourself," the beggar said, rattling the bowl. It didn't make much of a rattle.

"I'd offer you a quarter coil for directions, but somethin' tells me I've arrived."

The beggar's eyes widened. "You don't look like much of a gal. Unless you're hidin' some lipstick 'neath that mask."

"Don't have to be a gal to not want a demon child."

"Will ya shut your big bazoo then? You're supposed to drop a bean in the bowl. That's the signal."

Nox took out his pistol, holding it up. "Here's mine."

The "beggar" got up swiftly. He was surprisingly nimble for someone with a gammy leg.

"We've only got a few left," he said, glancing around. "Most of 'em are being bought up in Blackout. Too much demand and not enough product. How many you after?"

"I'm after a buyer."

"What? No. This is my turf here. You can sell your trinkets some place else."

"I ain't sellin' anything." Nox prodded the man in the shoulder. "But I'll buy some directions off you."

"You're some odd stick, you. Who're you after?"

"Goes by the name Handcart Sally."

"Sally Hays, huh? She's a right wagon, that one," the smuggler said. "Almost robbed me blind."

"Lucky I came then," the Coilhunter said. "I'm the law."

"I wouldn't give her no amulet for the price she was offerin'. Weren't no fairness in that. Sent her off to Harvey the Hound's jurisdiction on the other side of the Burg. She won't get a better price off him though, I can promise you that."

"This Harvey," Nox said, remembering the name, but not the face. "Has he got a setup like you?"

The smuggler laughed. "He's got a castle, more like. Got in good with the Barons. Almost one himself at this rate. It's only smuggler's law that doesn't got him pushin' me out o' the city altogether."

"Thanks," the Coilhunter said, casting a quarter coil into the bowl. He turned to leave.

"Wish you had been a gal!" the smuggler shouted after him. "I'd 'ave made more than that!"

"Here," Nox said, tossing something over his shoulder. It clinked in the bowl and rolled around. "A tip."

The smuggler looked inside. Right next to the quarter coil was a bullet.

Chapter Eight

THE SCENT

The Coilhunter made his way through the alleys, back out into the open trading plaza, stopping now and then to casually inspect some goods, make it look like he was buying, when he was just listening instead. He made his way to the other side of the city, following a trail of overheard words about the Dust Barons, until Harvey the Hound's name came up. It seemed he wasn't that popular with the traders, which was good for Nox, because bad news spread fast.

"Used to be one of us," a fishmonger said to one of the buyers. The fish were half-rotten by this stage, an import from Rustport far south. The reek of it probed even through the pores in the Coilhunter's mask.

"He was never one o' us," the buyer replied. "He was off galavantin' with the Scorpion's lot in the so-called 'Civilised South' for longer than he was up here fendin' off the heat like the Gosh-darn rest o' us."

Nox knew the name, and now the face as well. He'd met the Hound once before, back when he helped Taberah Cotten ("the Scorpion") hunt some ghosts. That wasn't quite as fun as hunting coils, and not half as satisfying as catching criminals. But Nox had been chasing ghosts of his own for a while now.

The problem with that was you tended to chase them into a grave. The Hound had a bit of knowledge about that too, but he was more a ghost-maker.

"Well, you make sure he gets the prime cut," the fishmonger said, "or he'll want a bigger cut of my wages."

Nox followed the buyer as he left the stall, but he barely had to keep an eye on the man. The smell left a pretty good trail of its own. The paper bag was already starting to burst open from all the oils and salts used as preservatives, not just to keep it fresh, but to seal in the flavour. The "taste of the sea" was a luxury this far into the desert, one that only someone like the Hound could afford.

The buyer halted suddenly, then turned around. Nox flung himself into an alcove, shoving his back against the wall. He winced as his guitar made a twang. He gave it a moment, then sniffed the air. It was a little fresher now, so the buyer must've set off again. Nox peered out, spotted the man, then shuffled after him.

"How much for that there six string?" a local asked him as he passed.

The Coilhunter barely glanced at him. "Your life."

Nox continued the pursuit, until he reached an unfamiliar part of the Burg. It looked like a new development, with stone that wasn't quite as well-kissed by the sun. But it was just as square and flat as the rest of the city.

There were guards outside the main complex, but the fish-buyer walked straight by them with ease. Nox strolled after him, but the guards blocked his advance.

"I'm with him," he said.

One of the guards looked at him, bemused. "No one goes with Smelly Scales."

Nox tapped the vent on his mask. "Why do you think I wear this?"

Before the guards could respond, a thick, green gas oozed from a little flask in the Coilhunter's hand, which he'd pulled from his belt as he reached for his mouth. The guards flopped to the ground and Nox stepped over them.

"Don't answer that."

He ambled inside, picking up the scent again. That dog sure loved his fish. It wasn't long before Nox had found his way into Harvey's inner sanctum, so much as it was. It wasn't all that lavish, but the idea of the Hound even having his own kennel was something Nox wouldn't have thought of only a year before. But there he was, sitting at the table, a face full of fur, with a bit of a wild look in his eyes.

"You," Harvey said, letting the slime of the fish fall from his mouth. He didn't even cook it. People said you'd dry up the sea that way. There must've been a lot of cooking to get that desert then.

"Me," the Coilhunter said, holding out his hands. The Hound was lucky he wasn't holding his guns.

"Well, whaddya know?"

"I know what's for dinner."

The Hound wiped his mouth with the back of his sleeve. He didn't look in the sharing mood. "Still chasing ghosts?"

Nox let out a puff of black smoke from his mask.

"Still chasing cats?"

"If the cats are amulet buyers, I've not just been chasing them. I've been catching them too. And catching coils while I'm at it." He patted his right pocket, which made a pleasant ching. "Looks like you're still hunting them."

"Oh, I'm huntin' all right, and it looks like I'm huntin' one of your dear pussies." He let the scroll unfurl, revealing her face and name.

"Ha!" the Hound barked. "Handcart Sally? You picked the wrong minx there, Nox. You could set a whole pack on her and she'd outrun them all!"

"But she isn't runnin' now, is she? She's here lookin' for you."

Harvey leant closer, letting the light show the bristles on his cheeks. "That's not how it works, Nox. I don't touch the goods myself any more."

That was a turn up for the books. When the Hound was smuggling directly for Taberah, he didn't want to share a bone.

"Things change, huh?" Nox said.

"They sure do."

"Well, don't change too much, Harvey. I wanna recognise ya when your face is on one of these posters."

The Hound smiled. "That'll be the day."

Nox smiled back with his eyes. "It sure will."

"I'll give you this one," Harvey said, "for old times' sake."

Nox almost scoffed. "For old times' sake."

"She's upstairs, with Grapevine Bill."

Nox tipped his hat, just a little. Harvey the

Hound didn't deserve any more than that. He left him to his meal, and let the stench filter out of his mask, replaced by the chemical odour he was used to from the tubes. There was something comforting in that, even though it often stung his lungs. Sometimes you didn't so much as survive the desert as limp on through.

He went upstairs, to where he saw young Grapevine Bill leaving a room carefully and quietly. Bill had some fascination with the Hound that was hard to explain, making him his lapdog. Sometimes you were just made to serve. And, in the Coilhunter's case, sometimes you were made to kill. When Bill spotted him, he scurried off, tail between his legs.

Nox pressed open the door Bill had come from, just as carefully, and even more quietly.

There she was. Handcart Sally. All locks and lashes. Her trademark blonde hair fell in waves upon her shoulders, and never seemed to dry up from the scalding sun. She wore a straw brimmed hat, with not a hint of make-up beneath. But she didn't need it. Even in her dungarees and soot-covered shirt, she had a rugged beauty about her. The image on her *Wanted* poster didn't do her justice. It was just a pity that the Coilhunter had to be that justice instead.

He stepped forward, ready to swoop in, but she turned and caught his gaze. It wasn't just animals that knew the scent of predator and prey. Humans knew it too. Before she'd even got a good look at him, she was out the door on the far side. She didn't stop to look back. You didn't survive in the Wild North by looking. You survived by running. So she ran.

And the Coilhunter followed. This was the part he liked the most. The hunt.

Chapter Nine

THE HUNT

Boy, she could run. She thundered down the corridor and leapt out of the window without a glance at what was below, tumbling on the cobblestones, and getting up just as quick. Then she was off again, down the street, zig-zagging between the crowd, hopping over the traders' tables like hurdles on a race track.

But the Coilhunter could run too, and dive and dodge just as well. He was after her like lightning, tearing his way through the throng of people, crashing his way over those same barriers, taking an accidental souvenir or two with him. The only reason he didn't brandish his gun was because he couldn't get a clear shot, because of the risk of some poor sod walking into the bullet.

So he ran.

And he soon realised that Harvey the Hound wasn't lying when he said she'd be hard to catch. The Coilhunter had his toys, his tools of the trade, but there was one thing you could count on with criminals in the Wild North: they'd cheat, steal, and kill for some of their own.

Mid-stride, Handcart Sally took an ornate,

copper pistol from her belt. Nox spotted it with his eagle eyes, and was ready with his eagle claws to fling some bullets of his own, but she didn't even turn to fire. She aimed it behind her, shooting a sprawling net at him, which he charged right into. He faltered for a moment, tearing his hand from the handle of his gun, and taking a knife instead from his belt. He sliced through the ropes, and the net fell down around him, catching on his ankle before he kicked it off mid-run.

Everything that Nox was carrying slowed him down a little, but even if it didn't, she wasn't just fast on the ground—she was fast on the walls as well. They turned into a tight alley, where she bounced her feet off one wall, then the other, criss-crossing her way up with ease, before hopping onto the roof.

Nox didn't even bother trying to scale the wall. He clenched his fist and shoved his arm up straight, triggering a mechanism in all the strapped-up wires running up his forearm, which fired a grappling hook to the top of the building. It latched into place, and yanked him upwards as the wire coiled tight. He grasped the rim of the roof and pulled himself up, tearing the grappling hook free, letting it recoil into its case.

Then he turned around and looked. She wasn't there.

"Damn!" he shouted, glancing around for some sign, some little dot of a figure dipping off into the sunset. Then he saw her, up on one of the higher roofs, leaping across to another, never stopping or slowing, never giving him a chance to catch up. You didn't get many chances in the Wild North, so you didn't give them to anyone either.

But he didn't need her. He'd make one for himself.

He fired the hook again and swung over to the higher roof, barely ripping the metal claw free from the tiles before he was off again. He didn't even get much of a run up before he threw himself over the gap between the buildings, only just clearing the chasm. He stumbled a little, but he didn't care, so long as he stumbled forward, towards the target, towards the kill.

There was a long stretch of level roofs ahead, with varying gaps between them. This was where she gained even more distance, her lean figure making her movements lithe. He trudged along behind her, making those same leaps, regaining a little speed of his own. He reached for the canisters on his belt, dislodging one mid-jump. It broke apart in an alley below, sending the gas out in all directions, and the civilians walking there into a pile on the ground. They'd be fine. Everyone could do with a nap every now and then. As soon as he landed on the other roof, he tossed a canister ahead of him, timed to explode right where she ran. But she must have heard him, or had some sixth sense, because she dived down into the next alley, letting the gas explode on the roof. Nox ran straight into it, and out the other side, breathing out his own black fumes from his mask.

He threw himself down into the alley, and just as she tumbled delicately, he crashed into the ground, before stumbling into the wall, taking a chip out of the brickwork. Yet just as quickly, she was back up the wall again, and onto the roof. He fired a token shot at her foot, just as it vanished over the edge, before aiming the grappling hook. It jammed. He couldn't afford to figure out what the problem was, so he ran towards the wall, simultaneously throwing a knife from his belt at the stone, where it lodged in place, and then another a little further up, and another higher still. He used them like stairs, dashing up the sides of the blades.

They were back on the level roofs, and this time Nox decided against using gadgets, in case she'd dive back down into the crowds again, and he'd lose more time trying to get back up. She already lengthened the gap, and showed no sign of slowing her relentless pace. That was the thing about knowing you were being hunted. You found some reserves of will and energy you didn't even know you had. But the Coilhunter had his own, and knew all about them. He didn't give up the chase so easily.

They approached the end of a set of roofs, which led to the outer wall of the city, and the deep dive down the plateau to the desert all around. He thought she was going to try to make that jump, crazy as it was, but she turned instead, setting off on another race across the next line of roofs. He wasn't sure where she was going, or if she was just trying to tire him out. He was getting tired, no doubt about it, but she could go for gold all she wanted; he was going for cold, hard iron.

In the charge, he noticed his monowheel like a toy far off to his right, parked outside the Dust Barons' jurisdiction. Then he saw why Handcart Sally took this route. Straight ahead, across many more rooftops, was a hang glider, a flimsy-looking contraption made of sticks and cloth. She dived straight into its harness, before running with it off the edge, letting the wind catch her.

Nox turned to his own form of gliding. He pulled a different kind of grappling device from his belt, firing one end into the nearby roof, and the other into the cliff-face far below, close to where he'd parked. Then he grabbed hold of the handles and curled his legs up, letting gravity pull him down the sloping wire, off the rooftops, across the city streets, over the city wall, and the vast drop below, right down to where he made a tumble in the sand, before hopping into the monowheel.

He started it up, scooping up the metal duck that stood guard nearby and casting it into the back. He took the binoculars from the front and stared through in the direction Handcart Sally had taken off. He saw her flying like a kite. So he bashed his boot down hard on the pedal, and set off to continue the chase across the desert, ready to reel her in.

Chapter Ten

CHASING KITES

The Coilhunter bolted off in his monowheel, sending out a huge plume of thick, black smoke behind him. The diesel engine purred and thrummed beneath him, and the wheel spun around him nice and brisk. He carved his way through the sand, the treads leaving their uniform print behind, while Handcart Sally cut through the clouds, leaving just a momentary blotch on the skyline.

He dove down dunes, letting gravity become his brief ally, even as it seemed to be doing nothing much to pull that woman down to her doom. He circled past a tall cactus here, or a small one there, flattening the desert brush, and evading the odd outcropping rock revealed by the shifting sands. He kept one eye on the changing terrain, though it didn't change much, and the other on his target in the sky.

"Come on, little bird," he said to himself. Even birds got tired and had to land. He just had to make sure the monowheel didn't tire out first. He had the extra diesel canisters on standby in case it got a little thirsty.

The wind started to grow, pushing her back a little, betraying her like it did to everyone sooner or later. The Coilhunter fell directly behind her for a moment, but she let a compartment of studded metal pieces open at the back of the glider. They tumbled down right into his path, creating a little minefield for him to traverse. They were packed too closely together for him to evade, and he was pressing the pedal too hard to slow or turn. He drove straight over them, rocking along the path, losing speed as the nails pierced straight through the metal treads. If it had been a tyre, he wouldn't have gotten far now— but this bike was adapted from the landships used in the war. It was made to take a beating. He was just a little surprised she was beating him at all.

She's good, he thought. Another one followed that he didn't like to think: that she was a bit like him, resourceful and cunning. Maybe that was where the comparison ended, or maybe she was also just as ruthless.

Yet, as much as he slowed, she couldn't keep her place in the clouds. She was already starting to dip a little. She was largely at the mercy of the winds, and they were rarely merciful. Nox could see her struggling to keep the glider in check, adjusting her position to turn it away from him, pulling on ropes and mechanisms to give it a little extra lift.

But there was no denying it. She was slowly coming back down to earth.

Nox drove alongside her, though she was still a good thirty feet up. She glanced down at him and scowled, as if to say, "You! You're *still* chasin' me?"

She kept her focus straight ahead, to where the sand gave way to some old abandoned mines, likely long plundered.

"You're better off surrenderin'," the Coilhunter rasped.

She didn't even look at him in response. There was no surrender at times like this. There was only living and dying. When the Coilhunter flipped the coin, it had death marked on both sides.

He answered for her with the swift draw of his pistol. He fired, and she cried out as the bullet hit her leg. The blood drizzled down her denim jeans and left a dappled trail in the sands—as if those grains needed to get any redder.

But she didn't give up or give in. One bullet wasn't going to cut it. It was rare that the Coilhunter had to use two.

He aimed the pistol again, and worked his fingers around the handle, getting that intuitive feel, that lucky rub that helped him get the final shot.

He fired.

The bullet streaked across the sky, but it didn't strike her. She threw her weight on one side of the glider and it spun full circle out of the way. Yet, in doing so, she lost even more height, and was now barely ten feet off the ground. She might as well have been running on foot.

And then she was.

She slipped out from the frame of the hang glider, dropping to her feet, and barely touching the ground before she sprinted off towards the mines. The wind yanked the glider back, then let it sail on its own course, winding and diving down near the monowheel, blocking his advance. It finally touched down right in front of the Coilhunter, and he drove straight into and over it, crushing the wooden beams, tearing through the cloth. He came out the other side, hot on Handcart Sally's heels.

He readied another shot. Some said a real man doesn't shoot a woman, but some said stealing and lying and cheating and killing weren't the roles of women either. Yet, maybe the Coilhunter wasn't a real man. Maybe he was something more. Maybe he was a nightmare the criminals couldn't wake up from.

It was too bad having a conscience. It was what separated him from them, but it was also what sometimes slowed his shots. He gave it a little too long, didn't give in to instinct, and by the time he had reasoned with himself, she had already dived deep down into the mines.

And while it was bad having a conscience, it was worse to let Handcart Sally retreat to the mines. That was her territory, just like the whole of the Wild North was his. He swept the sands for the scum, and she lived beneath them, where God-knows-what she did.

Chapter Eleven

HOME TURF

The Coilhunter never did like mines. There was something about going deep underground that made him feel on edge. Maybe it was the darkness. Maybe it was the odd sounds. Maybe it was because the further you went down, the harder it became to breathe. There was one benefit though: you got to hide from the blistering sun. The problem was: you didn't know what else was hiding with you.

Nox took a careful step into the blackness, keeping his hand ready by his waist, letting his eyes adjust. He knew he was giving Handcart Sally a lot of extra time this way, but she knew where she was going. When you were playing the game of life and death, sometimes you had to play it safe.

He crept in, slow and steady, watching the scree tumble, hearing the gravel crunch beneath his boots. There were far-off sounds like racing feet, or falling rocks, amplified by the acoustic channels of the man-made caverns. He sniffed out the smell of smoke, and spotted a few stray wisps from a newly-extinguished oil lamp hanging from the ceiling.

He carried on, banging his head off another just-snuffed lamp. She wasn't just trying to hide.

She didn't want him to see the way. That made him more cautious than ever. What he hated most was the thought that maybe it was just mind games, a way to slow him down for fear of phantoms.

Then he stepped on something that he knew wasn't gravel. His boot rocked on it, and he halted fast. He looked down, trying not to move his foot. It looked like rope, dusted over with sand and dirt. Sally hadn't disturbed it, because she knew where to run.

He waited for a moment, unsure if he should go back or press forward. He couldn't tell where the rope led, but he knew it couldn't be good. Reason told him she surely wouldn't light a fuse down here. You don't blow up the mountain when you're at the top. You don't strike the dynamite when you're deep beneath it either.

But she did.

He heard the sizzle of the fuse up ahead, coming towards him. Anyone else would have ran away from it, but he darted forward instead. That little spark of flame wasn't the problem. It was where it was going, to a pile of hidden dynamite near the entrance of the mine. She had the door rigged, and he wasn't just going to get shut in—he was going to get strewn apart.

He raced through the tunnel, following the sound, letting it guide him when the light wouldn't. He kept his arms out on either side, feeling his way, tripping now and then, and whacking his head twice off wooden beams used to support the roof.

He saw the glimmer of light approaching, and made for it. He stomped on the flame, trying to smother it, but it crawled through the cracks in his heel, a little weakened, but just as determined as ever to eat up the rest of the rope. He could have kept running, but he wasn't just here to catch Handcart Sally. He had to drag her body out as well. He couldn't do that if the entrance caved in.

So he leapt towards the fleeing fuse, dropping to the ground near it. He took out a knife strapped to his leg with the swiftness of any gunslinger and quickly severed the rope. He stood up, clutching the still-burning bit of twine. The flame travelled all the way down to his gloved fingers, where he snuffed it out.

"Boom," he said, letting the charred rope drop to the ground.

Then he paused.

Something didn't feel right. He moved the heel of his boot and felt something else. It wasn't the remnants of the rope, or the other bit still waiting for a light. It was another fuse, but it felt different. He didn't hear a light. Yet, on turning, he saw a barrel of TNT shoved into an alcove in the wall, masked by shadow. The fuse led straight up to it, and he'd bet his life that the other end had a switch. He might've had to cash in on that bet soon enough.

He ran, following the trail of the fuse, even as he heard the plunge of the detonator, and then the tremendous explosion behind him, which sent a fireball through the tunnel. The flames licked his heels, propelling him on. The chamber shook, and rocks dislodged from the ceiling, tumbling down all around him, striking his shoulders, grazing his legs.

He reached a larger cavern and dived, just as the passage behind him sealed off completely. The ground trembled for a moment still, then settled as he got to his feet. He saw the detonator there, turned on its side, as if whoever pressed it charged off before they'd fully pried their fingers from the handle.

She can't be far then, he thought. *She should've kept on runnin'.*

He looked around. There were three passages available, not counting the sealed one behind. Two of them had signs pinned above them: one a skull and crossbones, the other an exclamation mark on a triangular frame. Neither of them could be good. The third path had no label at all, but he couldn't be entirely certain if these were accurate indicators for true miners, or something a criminal like Handcart Sally came up with to lead bounty hunters astray.

He crouched down, dusting with his hand, looking for tracks. It seemed she'd covered hers well. What remnants there were seemed to lead to all three passages. Handcart Sally was good at running, but she didn't have six feet. She didn't have long before she'd be six feet under either.

"Come on, canary," he whispered. "Let me know which way you went."

He pulled a box from his belt and pressed the four buttons on all sides together. It opened, and out came a little mechanical bird. It fluttered there for a moment and landed on the index finger of his right hand. It looked at him with those same blank eyes he'd stuck on only a week back, but there was something about how it bobbed its head that made it seem like maybe it was alive.

"Find yourself a mate," he told it, hooshing it

away. It flapped in the air, cocked its head at him, then turned and looked at the three routes. Maybe it read the signs, and maybe it even made something of them, but it chose the middle path, more likely out of probability than anything else.

He repeated the process, pulling a second box from his belt. This was the last he had on him, so he couldn't scout out all three paths. This little birdie told him nothing, but it might as well have told him he meant nothing to it, for it took the left, unmarked path, leaving the one on the right—with the skull and crossbones—for its master.

"I guess it's fittin'," Nox said. He had the star of a sheriff on his breast, but as a bounty hunter, it might as well have been the skull and crossbones.

He took a step into the dark of that path, reaching up towards the sign as he passed. He pulled it down and let it drop to the ground, where the bones rocked for a moment, then went deathly still.

Chapter Twelve

THE BONE PATH

The passage was even more poorly lit than the previous one. It got a bit of natural light through a few cracks in the rock, but most of the light in this place came from the far-off glimmers of oil lamps. He saw one through a little alcove in the wall to his left, where he could also see his little mechanical canary going about its business.

He checked the tracker on his left wrist. The two red dots pulsed steadily, almost like a heartbeat. He'd put a lot of love into toys just like them in the good old days, right down to adding a little copper heart. But these ones? No. These didn't get to have one. They got to hunt out the beating hearts of others, and help put a stop to them too.

He reached what he initially thought was a dead end, but he spotted a tight gap in the corner, just big enough for someone as thin as Handcart Sally to squeeze through. He'd probably fit too, were it not for his equipment. He had to take his guitar off and pass it through first, and then the oxygen tank that was connected by tubes to his mask. It was lucky it was made fairly flat or he would have never got it in.

The tunnel here was darker, and it seemed the

wooden support posts were old. A few of them were rotten, and a few others had fallen over. But the roof still held—for now. He could have made a light of his own to guide his path, but that'd show him up too. It wasn't so bad being blind if your prey was blind too.

He continued on until he heard a crunch beneath his feet. He was glad it didn't feel like rope or wire, but he wasn't much relieved when he found out what it was. The ground was littered with bones, picked clean. You couldn't move without stepping on them, and hearing that awful crack. Something told him it was just Handcart Sally trying to scare him off. Another something told him it was something else.

The darkness made the little blinking red dots stand out more, so he noticed fast when one of them went out. That was the one that took the left, unmarked path. Something had got it. He probably should have taken that passage after all. This was the problem with gambles. Sometimes you lost.

He heard the sound of something like a lever, and froze. He looked around, barely seeing anything in the gloom. He grumbled as he was forced to pull a box of matches from his pocket and strike one. A little flame like that barely made a difference on most occasions, but in this pitch the difference was huge. He could see the shape of the walls and the winding passage, and the carpet of bones much more clearly. He could also see a pressure plate buried beneath them, and buried beneath one of his boots.

He sighed, and the smoke from his mask snuffed out the dwindling flame. He struck another and tried to get a better look at what he'd set in motion.

He didn't want to lean down too much, in case he'd inadvertently apply extra pressure, and he didn't want to ease up on the pressure he'd already placed. It didn't seem like this trap sprung when you stepped on it, or he'd probably already be dead. It was more likely it'd trigger once he lifted his foot.

He looked around for some rocks, trying to contain his growl as another match burned out. There wasn't much there within reach. The bones weren't much use either, not with the meat not on them. They didn't weigh a whole lot without it. He knew that well, as he sometimes had to let the carrion birds pick a body clean to lighten the load when heading back into town. Except the head, of course. He had to keep that intact for identification. If anyone complained that there wasn't much of a body left to go with it, he'd go with his usual retort: "Ya shoulda drawn more than a head on the poster then."

He looked back and noticed a large rock lining the path he had come from. He tried to reach for it, but it was just outside his grasp. He took his guitar off his back again, and used it to close the gap, with the curve in the wood and metal acting like a hook. He dragged the rock closer, then placed it down on the pressure plate.

He took a deep breath as he eased his own foot off. He could feel the plate shifting a little. That was probably fine, so long as it didn't shift a lot. He didn't even know what or where the trap was. He thought it better if he never found out.

The rock held the plate down, and he managed to step over it, strapping his guitar up again. He continued through the passage, barely getting ten careful paces before another match went out. He jumped when he felt a hand on his shoulder, turning sharply to it, gun raised. The faint light revealed a net hanging up on the ceiling, with two bodies inside, looking fresher than the rest, but still well dead. If this was Handcart Sally's work, then she was even worse than the poster said.

Suddenly, he heard a rush of sounds behind him. He turned, gun at the ready, but he barely saw anything before he felt a thump on his head, and everything went black. That wouldn't have been so bad, but it was in the blackness that he could see the fire.

Chapter Thirteen

THE SAWDUST SPARROWS

The Coilhunter wasn't used to going out cold, not even after a hard night at the prairie dew. When he came to, he wasn't just at sixes and sevens, he was mumbling to himself something frightening.

"I need to stop the fire," he said, still half in a daze. It took a moment for the blur to fade, before he could see Handcart Sally crouching down beside him, with a whole posse of good-for-nothings lined up behind her.

He tried to reach for his guns, but he felt the tug of the rope around his wrists, tied tight behind his back. There was nothing in the holsters at his waist. Hell, they'd taken every bit of a blade off him too. You couldn't blame them, even if you wanted to blame them with lead.

"Seems you was havin' a nightmare," Sally said, patting the mask on his face, as if to wake him up. He was surprised they hadn't removed that too. If they had, he'd probably already be dead.

Nox gave out a low growl. "Seems you're havin' one now," he said. "Difference is, you're starin' at it."

She let out a cackle. "D'ya hear this?" she said to the gang behind her. His vision was still too blurry to make them out proper.

Sally turned back to him. "Who sent you?"

"The Devil."

"You mean Blood Johnson? I told him I'd have his money this week."

"No," the Coilhunter rasped. "I was sent to bring you back to Hell."

She stared at him for a moment. "Who sent you?" she asked again, more aggressively.

"No one. I'm a lone wolf."

"Funny, that," she said. "So am I. Actually, scratch that. I ain't that lonely. I'm still a wolf though. Let me introduce you to the pack."

She stood up, clearing the way. When the Coilhunter wasn't focused on her, the rest of them came into vision, and he recognised them all. The Sawdust Sparrows. He had posters for them too. There was Cross-eyed Candy with her red straggles all twisted like brushwood, staring at him with one eye, while the other stared off somewhere else. Beside her, sitting just as bad as he was, was Limp-leg Trish, with her brown hair pulled back tight, which showed the soot on her face real good. Further on, there was Nine-finger Nancy, who was done up to the nines in guns and holsters, and only needed one finger to shoot them. They used to say you didn't face Nancy; you faced a whole damn arsenal.

Of course, they never did give themselves those names. They just stuck. The Coilhunter knew all about that.

And that was them, the Sparrows. All three of them, or so Nox thought. Normally gangs like that went down in number, because of him. Yet, normally he wasn't tied up by them either.

"Didn't take you for a Sparrow," he said. "Thought you were a wolf?"

She didn't like that. He knew she wouldn't. If you didn't have your guns, you still had your mouth. Of course, you had to be careful how you fired that off. He saw the fire in her eyes, and how hard it was for her to control it. She didn't like looking weak, not in front of the gang. She tried to keep her temper, show it didn't bother her, while deep down it gnawed away like a bullet.

Nox gestured with his head to the rest of them. "Quite a bunch you got here. Bit of a circus, even. You sure you belong? I mean, don't you have to have something wrong with you?"

"You'd fit in just fine," Trish said, pointing a blackened finger to his mask.

He smiled, knowing they couldn't see it, and let a puff of black smoke loose. "Well, I'm ready to join when you are. Just let me out of these bonds and I'll go sign the dotted line. Why, I'll even hoot and chirp for ya."

"He fancies himself a comedian, this one," Cross-eyed Candy said, holding up a serrated dagger. "I usually give those types a proper smile."

"Told you we should've slatted him silly," Nine-finger Nancy responded, spinning a revolver—his revolver—around her left index finger. She looked like someone who was more show than shot. Yet, the Coilhunter knew enough about her to know she liked to play with her victims, taunt them before killing them. And she'd killed plenty with the Sawdust Sparrows. Hell, that was how she got so many guns. Nox made a silent promise that she wouldn't get to keep his.

"If he moves," Cross-eyed Candy said, "you can do whatever you want with him. But keep him alive. We might get a nice ransom for him if he's got family that wants him still breathin'. We've got to sort out the heist. Keep an eye on him, will ya?"

She led Trish and Sally out, leaving the Coilhunter with the one-woman army of Nine-finger Nancy. All those guns probably kept most hostages quiet, but when two of them were his, Nox couldn't help but talk.

"You," he said. She perked up, pistols ready. He had that effect on people. They had the same effect on him. She stared at him, cold and silent, like how the barrel of a gun stared. It brought new meaning to the phrase *a murderous look*.

"You look like you've got some skill with those there six-shooters," he lied to her. She had a lot of six-shooters, but he couldn't see a hint of skill with them. With the others, he would've offered them a chance to make some chink, but she didn't seem that interested in coils. She was here for a different kind of metal, the kind with a trigger—and the thrill it gave.

She still didn't answer him. She was the silent type, the type you only heard with exploding gunpowder. With that many guns strapped to her breast, she didn't need good aim. Hell, she didn't even need luck. You only had to get hit by one lead pill and you were probably done for.

She was short of one digit, but she had a whole necklace of other people's fingers, so she didn't just collect guns. Some of them were long rotten, but others looked freshly cut. The Coilhunter didn't care much for the stories of demons down south, but he knew there were plenty of them just like her running around the Wild North.

"You ever find that missin' finger?" he asked her.

She looked at her right hand, where the index finger was cut to a stump. Some said she lost it in an accident, when she was playing soldier with a live grenade. Others said she was taught a lesson by the law, and they took her trigger finger to make her keep on learning. Those were the lessons the Coilhunter liked. Why, he was quite the teacher himself.

"I can help you make those hands a little even," he offered. It must've sounded like a tempting offer, even if it did come from him.

"How?" she asked.

"Ever heard of a game called Rock, Paper, Scissors?"

She looked at him, silent for a moment. "Yeah," she cawed.

"Well," the Coilhunter said, shifting in his seat, leaning a little closer, as if he was going to tell her a secret.

With a sudden swiftness, he leapt up, letting his worn-away bonds slip from his wrists. He grabbed one of the nearby rocks quicker than she could let off a shot, and bashed it against the side of her head.

"First, I use this rock," he said, as Nine-finger Nancy dropped to the ground. "Then I take this paper with your face on it." He unfurled the Wanted poster, letting her see what the law looked like, in black and white, before the red got into her eyes. "And then I find me some scissors." He pulled one of his daggers from her collection and squatted near her as she spasmed on the track, holding up her good hand. "And I make this hand match that one. Then you'd be Eight-finger Nancy. But that doesn't quite roll off that tongue, does it? So, we'll leave you with all nine. But ya see, you should've taken a better look at that poster. It don't say Alive or Maimed. To me, it don't even say Alive."

He pulled a pistol from one of the holsters strapped to her, and fired faster than she could dream of firing. She went out cold. Some called it a mercy shot, but for types like her, he hadn't got much mercy. That was the thing about the Wild North. The desert tended to dry up everything, even the good stuff. Your compassion, your conscience—it didn't matter. It all blew away like dust.

He heard approaching footsteps and put his back to the wall near the door. He waited, wondering if they'd spot the body first, and run away, or run straight into his waiting gun. He heard a muted gasp, then a rush of boots. In popped Handcart Sally with her luscious locks and pale, soot-stained skin.

Nox pointed his pistol and cocked the hammer.

"Any last words?"

"Wait!" she cried. "I know what happened to Waltman."

Chapter Fourteen

KNOWLEDGE IS A
DANGEROUS WEAPON

"I'm listening."

She took a moment to compose herself. It was one thing to blurt something out when you felt the barrel against your temple. It was quite another to say something with intent, to string all those spilling words together into proper sentences.

He decocked the hammer. It was like giving her tongue back.

"He was lookin' for you," she said. "He came lookin' when he shouldn't have been lookin'."

"So you killed him?"

"No! I didn't kill nobody. Not in my whole life."

"There are a whole lot of posters out there that say otherwise."

"Yeah, and they don't always say the truth."

She was right there, but that didn't mean she was right about herself.

"Go on," he said, nudging her with the barrel.

"He said he knew something you'd want to know. He said it was urgent."

"Why did he tell *you* this?"

"He didn't. I was told it later."

"By whom?"

"Blood Johnson."

"The debt collector?"

"That's puttin' it mildly."

"What did Blood Johnson want with Waltman?"

"He wanted him dead. He said he was told by his … his superior … that Waltman had to go."

"His superior," Nox mused.

"Yeah." She turned her head to him, ignoring the risk, until the barrel pointed straight between her eyes. "I think that's the man you're lookin' for."

It was such an odd feeling to lose his grip on the gun. It almost slipped. It almost fired too. He could kill a snake in the brush from a hundred yards, a skill honed by years of practice, years of discipline. Yet here he was, barely able to hold the weapon tight.

"He was in a carriage," she said, "and Blood Johnson was talkin' to him. He had a deep, rough voice, like granite. I didn't get to see him. I think he only came to make sure the job was done."

"What job?"

"Burying Waltman."

The Coilhunter took a deep breath. The deeper he took them, the blacker the smoke that came out of the exhaust. It was quite a concoction in that drum upon his back. He wasn't just breathing in oxygen now.

"I didn't kill Waltman," she said. "He was already dead before I was called in. Blood Johnson made sure of that."

"So, why'd he call you?"

"That's what I do. I get rid of bodies. I put them

places no one'll find 'em. That's why they call me Handcart Sally. I load those poor souls up in the handcart and bring 'em out to the wastes, to where even the sun don't dare go. But I don't kill 'em myself. I ain't never hurt a fly."

"But you wrapped them up for the spiders though."

"I ain't proud of what I do."

"Good. You shouldn't be."

"He makes me do it, y'know. Blood Johnson. It started with one loan, and then it kept gettin' higher. I can't shake it, and I can't shake him. No matter what I do, I always seem to owe him some. It's like he doesn't really want me to pay it all off. He *owns* me. So, when he tells me I need to hide something for him, I have to go and hide it. And I just went and done something stupid, got another loan. But it wasn't for me this time. It was for … a friend."

"The things we do for friends," Nox said.

"That's why I got in with the Sparrows. We was lookin' to rob some people on the road. Then I could clear my debts and get away from all this."

"Get away from all this." Nox shook his head. "It ain't that easy."

A tear rolled down her cheek. "I know."

"Even if I pull this trigger, you'll still owe those debts."

"I know," she whispered.

"Well, you owe me something, that's for sure. You can bring me to where you buried Waltman. And if you're lucky, and I find out from his ghost what his livin' self was gonna tell me, then maybe I won't ask you to dig another one of those graves you're so good at diggin'. Maybe I won't ask you to dig it for yourself."

Chapter Fifteen

A DEAL

The Coilhunter never lowered his gun. He'd done that before, back in the early days, and he had a few scars for it. She mightn't have been a killer, but she didn't need to kill him to beat him, and she didn't need him dead to bury him. This whole network of mines was one big burial ground just waiting to happen.

He tied her wrists behind her back, using the barrel of the gun to help wrap the knot. It was important that they kept feeling the touch of the steel, cool or scalding hot, to help keep them in line. There were a lot of threats with words in the Wild North, so much so that they didn't quite mean anything—but if you made the threat with the touch of steel, well, that meant everything.

"Keep steady," he warned her. "You don't want my hand to slip."

"I ain't gonna run," she told him.

Nox scoffed. "That's all you've been doin'. It's kind of like askin' the desert not to be dry."

He finished the knot, testing that it was tight.

"They'll be back for me, y'know," she said. If she were wise, she would've kept her mouth shut. Then again, if she were wise, she wouldn't be in with the Sawdust Sparrows in the first place.

"They can come back, but you won't be here."

She turned her head to him, eyes wide.

"You ain't just tellin' me the way," he said. "You're showin' me."

"No. I've gotta finish this job. I gotta get the money. I've gotta pay off my debts and get outta here. I can't afford no diversions. I can't afford—"

"You can't afford to say no. You got lucky today. Fate's given you a second chance. You should take it, gal, 'cos I won't be givin' you a third."

She said nothing. It wasn't quite a "yes," but it wasn't "no" either. She'd likely try to break free on the road, but he'd be watching her. Yet he knew he needed something else. Some people were too used to the nudge of a gun. They weren't quite used to the dangling carrot.

"Here," he said, turning her around and nudging up her chin. "I'll make you a deal. You help me find out what Waltman wanted me to know, and I'll help clear your debt with Blood Johnson."

She blinked at him. "You'll pay my debt?"

"Hey, I didn't say anything about payin'. Well, not with iron anyway." He spun his revolver around and slipped it in its holster.

"He's a hard man to kill."

"Good. I like a challenge."

They heard a sudden howl from further back in the mine shaft.

"What was that?" he asked.

"I don't know."

"Didn't sound like no Sparrow."

"No."

"You holdin' out on me, gal?"

"Trish said there was something else that lived down here."

"Like what?"

"I dunno. Monsters."

"And you believed her?"

They heard another howl.

"I believe her now."

Chapter Sixteen

MONSTERS IN THE MINES

They heard screams from one of the tunnels. A lot of screams.

"That sounds like Candy," Sally said.

It was followed by growling and grunting, and the kind of noises nothing known to either of them made.

"That don't sound like her," Nox added.

They both instinctively took a short step back.

"These monsters," Nox said. "What're they like?"

They stepped back again. Nox kept his hand hovering near the holster.

"I don't know. They never said. Just that they were there, somewhere, sleepin'." She looked at him. "You went down the Bone Path, didn't you? That's where we pulled you out. I think … I think you might've woken them up."

They fell silent, focusing all their attention on the tunnel ahead, letting their minds create all kinds of horrors.

Then something emerged from the shadows of the tunnel. It was a huge, hulking figure, with bulging limbs, walking on its shell-covered knuckles. It had a face of knives, teeth long enough to spear you whole.

It had three eyes, but they were small, as if maybe it didn't need them in the dark. It sniffed loudly, and as soon as it caught their scent, it bounded towards them, rocking the chamber as it went.

Nox had both pistols out before it made the second quake, and three rounds each off before it made the third. It gave out its terrible howl through the tiny gaps between the bladed cage of its teeth, then crashed to the ground at the Coilhunter's feet.

Sally opened her clenched eyes.

Nox smiled with his own. "Time we put 'em back to bed."

The cave shook, and they heard the thump of knuckles, and the smaller, frantic patter of feet.

"You got enough bullets for them all?" Sally asked.

Nox knew he didn't. He was out hunting one woman, not an army. He looked around, spotting Nine-finger Nancy and her blood-spattered arsenal. He rummaged through the straps and holsters, pulling out a few guns.

"Nox!"

The pounding and patter grew louder. Limp-leg Trish raced around the corner, struggling to run with her bad leg. One of the creatures came after her, playing the ground like a drum. Then Trish slipped, just before she got to their chamber. She fell flat on her face and looked up at them with desperate eyes, even as the creature hovered over her.

"Help me!" she screamed as the monster grabbed a hold of her ankle and started to pull her back.

Nox let loose two rounds from the newest

pistol he'd unearthed from Nancy's array, but then it jammed. The creature bellowed in response, but kept on tugging.

"Damn," Nox said, casting the gun aside. He tried another, but it was blank. Half of these were just for show. But somewhere on her, in some of those cases, or behind some of those straps, were the rest of his weapons.

Trish's screams as she was dragged away were deafening.

"Help her!" Sally shouted.

He flipped his good pistol up and rolled out the barrel. Just one bullet left. He sighed and flicked it back into place. He had to make it count. He pointed it towards the tunnel, closing one eye. With the other, he could see Trish tilling the ground with her fingernails. He could also see the giant shadows of more of those lumbering beasts coming up behind.

Then he fired, sending the bullet straight into Limp-leg Trish's forehead. She stopped screaming and fighting and tilling, and the creatures pulled her away, before they pulled her apart. It was all he could do to help her now. There were too many of them, and not enough bullets. He used to say that about the criminals. And here was one of them, standing at his side, and he had no more pebbles in his gun.

"Come on," he said, pulling Sally by the arm. "We need to get outta here."

Sally didn't say anything. You could see a lot in the Wild North, but you never saw everything. Most things faded away, but some left a burn on your brain. You could wash your mind a thousand times, but you'd never get those images out.

He tugged her more forcefully, until she almost stumbled over. He caught a glimpse of her eyes, wide with shock, wet with that little oasis of tears. He knew that look well. He saw it in a thousand faces. And when he dared look in a mirror, he often saw it in his own.

He grabbed his guitar and tossed it into one of the nearby mine carts. It twanged insultingly in response. He looked for his rifle. It'd usually be strapped to his back, but it seemed it was strapped to Nine-finger Nancy's instead. He was lucky she wasn't wearing his fingers as well.

"You're not seriously thinkin' of ridin' in that thing," Sally said, nodding towards the mine cart. It was black with coal, and beneath the soot there was probably rust. The tracks didn't look a whole lot healthier either. It seemed like they went on forever, into the gloom.

Nox wrestled with Nancy's body, trying to pull free his rifle. For a dead woman, she could wrestle well. "I … don't … think … we have a choice."

The growls and grunts came again, followed by the quakes. The shadows of the creatures appeared on the walls of the tunnel behind them.

Sally didn't need to be told to get in. She hobbled over to the cart, leant her belly against the edge of it, and let gravity tilt her forward until she fell inside with a clang. When she sat up again, her face was even more soot-stained than it was before.

"Nox!" she cried.

The creatures were now in the chamber, spreading

out around the outer walls, surrounding them.

"Start her up!" the Coilhunter shouted back.

Sally struggled in her bonds. "I can't!"

Nox dropped Nancy's body for a moment and ripped the last remaining canister from his belt, flinging it towards the nearest creatures. It burst, and there was a bang, followed by a flash of white that left a sting in the eyes. It was debilitating beyond measure, and the Coilhunter had to rely on feel as he attempted to root out some good guns from Nancy's corpse. When the light faded, Nox realised something: not one of the creatures gave a howl at the glow. It didn't affect them at all. They were essentially blind. Just like Nancy's guns, the eyes were just for show.

"You shoulda freed me," Sally groaned.

Nox gave another tug of the rifle, but it wouldn't come loose. "Hell," he said, then grabbed Nancy by the shoulders and started to pull her with him.

"What're you doin'?" Sally cried.

"Gettin' my guns," he grunted.

"Leave 'em!"

The nearest creature darted forward. The Coilhunter barely had time to let Nancy's body slump and his own hands reach around to one of the weapons before it was almost on him. He felt the trigger and heard the click, but there was no blast. Just as quickly, he kicked the body forward until the head drooped down, exposing the barrel of his rifle, still stuck to Nancy's back. He cocked it quick and let it rip.

The creature snarled and screamed, and limped back, wounded. It made a series of noises, a mix of gasps and clicks, which seemed to be repeated by the others, and they all seemed wary now.

That's right, Nox thought. *Now you know the fire burns.*

He grabbed the body again and quickly dragged it across to the mine cart, standing it up and hauling it in, until Nancy was poised upon a pile of coal, both legs and arms dangling over the edge. He hopped inside after her, kicking out a few stray lumps of coal.

Sally looked at him, her eyes as wide as ever. "You got no respect for the dead?"

"Oh, I do, but you gotta pay your respects to the living." He shoved Nancy's body over a little to make room for his own. "And you're one to talk, Corpsecart Sally."

He reached for the lever outside the cart and pulled it tight. The wheels creaked into motion, grinding against the tracks. Then it started to roll forward, away from the gathering monsters. They seemed to be continuing their obscure dialogue. Nox wasn't sure what they said, but he imagined it was some variation of: "Don't let the dinner get away!"

Chapter Seventeen

ON THE RAILS

The mine cart creaked on the tracks, the wheels grinding as they spun, the rust crunching apart as iron slammed against iron. This was a hand-powered vehicle, with two alternating hand-levers that needed to be pushed and pulled on either side. The Coilhunter worked them now, and the cart chugged up a slope, before plummeting down again on the other side. Then Nox could let gravity do some of the work.

"Where does this lead?" he asked.

Sally shimmied into place, letting the coal topple around her. She shrugged. "I dunno."

"I thought mines were your desert," Nox said. "Thought you knew every grain of 'em."

"Yeah, well, you think a lot of things about me, and ain't none of 'em true."

"They ain't all a lie either."

She glared at him. "And what about you? Are the things they say about you all true?"

"Depends what they say."

"That you're just as bad as the people you hunt."

His chest heaved, and he exhaled a puff of dark smoke. "I hunt killers."

"You *are* a killer."

"I only kill the worst of the worst."

"Why don't you go and put that gun to your head then, cowboy?"

He was silent again for a moment. "This place needs a lawmaker."

"We make our own laws here."

"Yeah, like the loan shark laws that got you into the mess you're in. And hell, they're different for every shark. You wanna swim in those waters, then be my guest, but there's a lotta drownin' people out there, bein' pulled under no less. Someone's gotta do something."

It was her turn to be silent. It was easy to talk about frontier freedoms, but they came at a price. If you wanted no laws for the good, you had to give them to the bad as well. Things got pretty ugly then.

"Nox!" Sally cried, waving her bound wrists.

He turned, and saw something approaching from the gloom. It was another kind of cart, but this one was powered by several of the creatures from before, and it had a large mining drill on the front, spinning wildly as it came near.

Nox pumped down on the levers, working his arms furiously. The drill cart came dangerously close, the tip of the drill grazing the sole of one of Nancy's boots. Then the Coilhunter managed to pick up the pace, pulling away from it before she became No-leg Nancy too.

He pulled and pushed with a frenzy, as if pulling his life back, and pushing theirs away. His muscles spasmed from the sudden intense force of it all. He could feel the lumps of coal digging into his legs. He could feel the whoosh of the stale, tar-tinted air on the back of his neck. He could see the monstrous faces of the creatures approaching, and hear the monstrous spinning of the drill.

He pressed his knees together over Nancy's body, catching the handle of a pistol between them and yanking it from its holster. As soon as it was free, he grabbed it and fired three times. Two bullets landed in the head of one of the beasts, but the third strike of the trigger just gave out a click. He tossed the gun over the edge, down into the deep darkness below, where it seemed to keep on falling. Just as quickly, he brought his hand back to the lever, back to the pushing and pulling.

"Free me and I'll work the cart," Sally said from behind him. He could feel her eyes boring into his skull as if she was a drill of her own.

He said nothing, reaching for another gun with his heels. He couldn't get a good grip on it.

"Or free me and I'll work the guns," Sally added.

"Never in your life." The problem with promises from the con artists was that they were far too often just another con.

"Well, maybe in your death then," she said. "Might come soon enough."

He grumbled as the gun slipped between his heels again. The focus on it had slowed his pumping arms, and now the drill cart came a little closer.

He growled, grabbing a dagger from his boot and tossing it behind him, where it cleaved a lump of coal in two. "Try and stab me with that and I'll throw you over."

He heard the tumble of coal as she shifted in place, and then the rub of metal against rope as she cut through the bonds. He half-expected to hear the rush of the blade coming towards him, or feel the sting of the metal in his side. He didn't expect what happened: she fired the dagger with incredible force and speed at the driver of the drill cart, landing the blade straight in its forehead. The creature grunted, then toppled over the edge of the vehicle.

"Damn," the Coilhunter said. "Kind of wish I hadn't left my other daggers at the Burg now."

She placed her hand on his, working the right lever. "Let me drive. I think we need you shootin.'"

She was right. Even as the drill cart slowed, another of the creatures took over, speeding it up again. And now several other tracks ran parallel on either side, and on some of them were more carts of various shapes and sizes, filled with more of the monsters, some with guns and daggers of their own.

Nox let Sally take over, while he rummaged through the arsenal wrapped to Nancy's body. He pulled his rifle loose, filled it with a few fresh rounds, then began taking out the creatures one by one, until there were no more bullets left in it, and none left in his pockets or on his belt.

He shoved the rifle into a strap on his back, then switched to the next gun Nancy's ghost had ready for him. There was only one round in the barrel, but he made it count, knocking away an incoming blade. It was like target practice all over again. Except usually he shot the objects up into the sun-seared sky, and when they came back down again, they only came from one direction. Right now, the monsters were firing things from all sides, forcing Nox to duck and dodge, and pull Nancy's body up like a human shield.

"We need more speed," he urged.

"I'm tryin'."

"Well, try harder."

"We need more guns," she said.

Nox looked at the two dozen more weapons strapped to Nancy. "Guns ain't the problem." He fired another, but there was nothing in it. "We need bullets."

He heard Sally gasp, and turned momentarily to see an intersection of the tracks. On the far end of the horizontal one crossing theirs was another cart, this one with a scooper attached to the front. It was meant for clearing debris from the tracks, but the monsters meant it for them.

"I think I need to slow down," Sally said.

"No! The drill's gaining on us." Nox focused his fire there. He even threw the spent guns onto the tracks, hoping they'd jam in the wheels, but most of them fell through the gaps.

"They're gonna crash into us!" Sally cried.

The scooper cart trundled down towards them. It had a larger stretch of track to cover, but it came from a slope, so its speed was faster. From the looks of it, they would strike each other soon. Sally could have slowed down to avoid them, but the drill would've pushed them on, if it didn't tear them apart first.

"Give it hell," Nox said, joining her on the levers. They took one each, putting all their strength into it. The wheels screeched and the track wailed. The monsters made lots of horrible noises of their own. And still the hail of objects came, striking the sides of the cart or sailing over it as Nox and Sally bowed low.

They could see the scooper cart real close now, almost close enough to feel the edge of the shovel lift them off the tracks. But they gave it hell, and sped past by a matter of inches, while the scooper caught the side of the drill cart and hauled it up off the tracks, sending it over the edge.

The parallel tracks split apart, and the monsters fell back into the darkness, still hungry. Dinner was never so much hard work.

Nox and Sally didn't take their sudden solitude for granted. They kept working the levers for what felt like hours, taking turns, barely getting much rest at all before they had to take it up again. Eventually, they saw the pinprick of light from the outside world and headed towards it. It was strange to curse that skin-sweltering sun before, and yet pray for it here—but as soon as they came out into the glow and glare of it again, the old curses came back with a vengeance. The old Coilhunter came back with a vengeance too.

Chapter Eighteen

THAT UNFORGIVIN' SUN

Nox never did like the sun, and it seemed the feeling was mutual. His skin was already creased and cracked, and the brim of his hat only helped a little. The light got in everywhere, and the heat did too. You couldn't run from it, and you couldn't hide from it for long. It would be there, waiting for you the next day.

They were barely out of the mines when the Coilhunter slung a line of rope around Sally's wrists again, though this time she was allowed to keep them in front of her.

"So much for teamwork," she said.

He made a noose with another line of rope and hooked it over her neck, before tightening it. She coughed in protest.

"Get used to it," he said. "This ring of yarn might be the last thing you feel."

"Some men buy a gal a ring for her finger, y'know."

He tipped his hat to her. "I wouldn't hold out hope."

"It ain't always a drug. There's some real good here, even in the Wild North, beneath the sand."

He scoffed. "It's always a drug, 'specially the

94

dreamy stuff."

They'd gone so far in the mines that they weren't sure where they'd come out. His monowheel was nowhere to be seen. He hammered the tracking device on his left wrist, but it was busted up right and proper. The Sparrows had taken a lot of his tools off him, leaving his belt a lot lighter than he liked it. His spare tools were in the monowheel.

"We'll have to walk," he said.

"I gathered that."

Nox started off, with Sally in tow. He could've trusted her, maybe, but he'd spent his trust like he'd spent those bullets. That was one way the bad guys won. They made you doubt the good.

It was about midday, which was when the sun was fiercest. People usually went inside then, and for a brief moment—an hour or two—the Wild North didn't seem so wild. The criminals needed their siestas too.

"What made you like this?" Sally asked as she stumbled through the desert after him.

He said nothing.

"You don't just become someone like you."

He kept silent, wishing she would too. Some slung their tongues as fast as he hit the trigger. The Coilhunter wasn't much of a talker. He liked to keep things short and sweet, just like the lives of criminals. Well, the short bit anyway. Out here in the desert, the air was hard to come by, so for the most part he kept his breath for breathing. Hell, he kept a whole drum of it strapped to his back.

"I need … to rest," she said.

"No." He pulled her up as she began to slip down. "We need to keep going." His own breath was laboured now. He barely had enough energy to move his own limbs, let alone drag hers.

The heat haze made everything shimmer. The grit of the ground seemed to blur into the glimmers of the sky, until they weren't sure where they were walking, nor in what direction.

"There's water!" Sally cried, though it was a hoarse cry. She pointed her bound hands ahead.

He didn't see it. The cynicism in him helped against the illusions of the sun, as did a lot of experience. He'd ran to many mirages in the past, and there were no oases out there. If you drowned in the Wild North, you drowned in the desert. You'd be lucky if you got a sup of water at all.

"Here's your oasis," he said, tossing her his water canister. It was hot from the sun, and there wasn't much left in it, but she gulped it down all the same. She didn't have the energy to throw it back to him.

"We're going to die out here," she said. She might have cried if she could afford the tears.

"Maybe your ghost can bury us somewhere no one'll find us."

She said nothing. Maybe she had a conscience after all. That was rarer than water out here.

They staggered onwards, down the dip of dunes, struggling up others. The sun creaked along the tracks of the sky slowly, burning one side of them before moving on to the other, making sure they were nice and crisp all over. Maybe the monsters'd come back and find them cooked.

When the day started to wane, and Sally stopped asking questions about his past, they could see a faint red glow on the horizon which wasn't the setting sun.

"What's that?" Sally asked. "Can you see it? Is it another mirage?"

"I can see it," he said. "That ain't no mirage. That's the Ruby District."

"Well, I hope you kept your coils, Coilhunter, because that'll be as dried up to us as the desert is without 'em."

"Not to me, it won't," he said. "But don't you worry, Handcart Sally." He rattled his pocket, where the coils clinked together. "That's our real oasis ahead."

Chapter Nineteen

THE RUBY DISTRICT

The Ruby District was one of the more welcoming parts of the Wild North—if you had coils to spare. If you didn't, well, it just didn't exist. You'd see it like a red haze on the horizon, and you'd never get far enough to see the hue up close. If you were lucky, you'd overhear a tale or two in one of the saloons. If you were really lucky, you got to tell them too.

It was run by Ruby Down, an enterprising woman who came out into the wild long before many others, and staked her claim to these parts. She promised other enterprising women a world of opportunity, though most of the opportunity was for herself. She advertised her little kingdom as a land of opportunity for everyone else, so long as you came loaded, and left empty. Some of those cowboys telling tales across bars were getting paid by her—though not always with money.

The Ruby District was a paradise for many, with all the sin of Hell mixed with the ecstasies of Heaven. There was little you couldn't buy there, and no dream or pleasure Ruby Down wouldn't procure. She charged high and paid well, but while you were enjoying your own naughty pleasures, someone else was enjoying something you didn't quite like next door. But most people turned a blind eye to that. Both eyes were usually pretty busy staring at something else.

Nox hauled Sally into the makeshift town, with all its red canopies and lampshades. He got a look or two from a few of the locals, who spotted Sally's bonds and smiled. Nox quickly realised that maybe that sent the wrong signal. Sally was having her bonds cut a lot lately. It wasn't like him. Then again, it wasn't every day he got a clue to his family's killer.

He ushered Sally ahead of him now, watching for a quick move. She was so exhausted she could barely move at all, and he had to catch her once or twice. A group of scantily-clad women frolicked over with lemon water. That was ecstasy enough for the thirsty.

Once they'd gained a bit of composure, Nox led Sally into the main building, where the District's proprietor could always be found, come rain or shine. Well, come shine anyway.

Ruby Down. What could you say about her? Quite a bit, if she'd let you. She'd been around a while, long enough for the colour in her hair to fade. They might have been grey locks, but they were thick and bushy still, and the lace of jewels she wore over it gave it all the colour it needed. Her face was worn, like most faces, but it had gained a kind of authoritative definition, like the craggy outcrops of the desert canyons. They didn't just communicate age, but said: here we've stood the test of time, and will stand forever more. She was plump, having abandoned the hard labour and sweat of her youth for the luxury of life in the Ruby District. She smoked heavily, and drank heavily. There wasn't much she did in small measures. "Go big or go home" could have been her motto, if she had any time for mottoes.

"Well, well, well," she said, her voice equal parts allure and the hoarseness of age and cigarette.

Nox tipped his hat to her. "Howdy."

"I've not seen you in quite a while." She flicked through her desk calendar, but he wasn't on any of that year's dates.

"I've been busy."

"So I heard. You're working up quite an enterprise at the Bounty Booth. Giving me a run for my money, even." She paused, then tapped a giant signet ring off the table. "Killing off some of my customers too."

"If I killed 'em, they deserved to die," Nox croaked.

"You know me. I don't go in for moralising. One man's crime is another man's pleasure. That's how it works in the Ruby District. You know the rules, Nox. You leave those man-made laws at the door."

"I know the rules," the Coilhunter said. "Those Ruby-made rules, little laws of their own."

She ignored him, turning her attention to Sally. "Now, you're a specimen! Lookin' for work, girl? You'd fetch a fair price in here."

"She's already got a job," Nox said.

"And someone to speak for her, it seems."

"I can speak fine for myself," Sally said. "I'm just … passin' through."

Ruby laughed boisterously. "*Everyone's* just passing through, girl. Sure, isn't that the nature of life, itself? It's what you do while you're passing that's of interest here. Or maybe … maybe you're looking for a little something yourself? We've got all types for all types. You name it, we have it—or we'll find it for you."

Sally looked around awkwardly at some of the "walking merchandise" on display. There certainly were a mix of types there, though Ruby kept some of the more "exotic" interests in different rooms.

"I'm good," Sally said.

Ruby chuckled. "There's nothing good about you. I can see that plain. I'd even peg you as one of Nox's poster girls if you weren't still standing. You've got the look of trouble about you. Well, girl, there won't be any trouble here, you mark my words." She slapped her hand down on the table hard and it rocked from the force. "Or I'll mark something else."

"Don't you worry about her," Nox said. "I'll take care of her."

Ruby raised an eyebrow. "You do what you want, but the only bangs I want to hear are the sounds of bedposts against the wall. You can leave the pistols with me."

Nox took a little pouch from his belt and placed it on the table. "One hundred coils. Well, it might be a few short, what with the road not being a road and all."

Ruby emptied the bag out and started sorting the pieces into wholes, halves, and quarters. She had an efficiency about her, like pistons pumping. The patrons came for all sorts, but counting coils was one of her little pleasures.

"We need somewhere to sleep," Nox said, "and I *mean* sleep."

"You could live here for a month on this."

"I only need a night. But I need supplies too. Stuff for the road."

"The Coilhunter with no supplies? Now, there's a sight. You must have left in a hurry. Why didn't you get them at the Burg? They'd be cheaper there, even with the tax."

Nox looked at Sally. "I was preoccupied."

Ruby scooped away each stack of coils. "Well, you'll need to tell me what you need. I've got limited supplies here too. The Dust Barons have upped the taxes, so I've been trying to get some from Blackout, but there are muggers on the road south, so I lose a lot there too."

"I'll see to the muggers in time," Nox said. He took a piece of paper out and handed it to Ruby.

"This is all you want? For a hundred coils?"

"I ain't lookin' for much here. What I'm lookin' for is out there in the desert."

"Whatever you say, Nox."

"And the extra coils. Well, they're to let me keep my guns."

She rolled her eyes, as if she expected him to say that. "If you keep them holstered."

"If those are the rules," he said.

"They are."

"Then you know me."

"Yes," she said, smiling. "Isn't that the problem?"

"Depends who you are."

"Maybe keep them more than holstered. Wrap them up. Put a skirt on or something. Guns don't go down well here. They spook the guests. Then again, you spook them too."

Nox smiled behind his mask. "Good."

He turned to leave, but Sally loitered for a moment.

"Ruby," she said.

"Yes, girl? You changed your mind about something?"

"No. Well … yes. I'm looking for a woman."

"I knew it!" Ruby said, turning to Nox. "I can peg them from a mile away." She hoisted herself up and ambled over to a chest of drawers, from which she pulled a giant folder full of drawings and black and white photographs, with names and attributes, and sexual likes and dislikes. She plopped it on the table. There wasn't a speck of dust that came from them. They had been well rifled through at this stage.

"Now," Ruby said. "You have a look through those and see if there's any who meet your fancy. That's not all of them, mind you, as we have a few new ones who aren't on the books yet. We're giving them a trial run."

Sally paused. "Can I see the new ones?"

Ruby's eyes widened. "She knows what she wants, this one!"

She hobbled off again, clapping her hands together, as if she considered herself the desert's matchmaker. In a way, she was—though the matches didn't last for long.

"What are you doing?" Nox whispered to Sally.

"Just … blending in. You should try it."

Nox raised his eyebrows. "I blend in fine."

Sally tapped her hand against either side of his mask. "You keep tellin' yourself that, hun."

103

"Here we go!" Ruby erupted. She led them through into another room, yelling for "Ulla!" repeatedly, until a very thin woman, almost the mirror image of Ruby, came down the stairs.

"What's all this yellin' about?" she asked.

"Get us the newbies, will you, love? The girls, that is."

"The women," Sally interjected. "Only the women."

"Some of 'em are *indisposed*, so they are," Ulla said, yawning mid-sentence.

"Well, get the ones who aren't!" Ruby shouted. "We've got some special guests tonight."

Ulla went away, leaving the three of them standing in the room below. Nox looked awkwardly at the other two, while Sally feigned a smile. Ruby was the embodiment of excitement, pacing to and fro, rubbing her hands together briskly, periodically exclaiming "oooh!" and "wait till you see them!"

Eventually, Ulla returned, leading a train of women behind her. There were eleven in total, some pale, others with dark skin, some tall, others short. If Sally had really been looking for a companion for the night, she had a good mix to choose from. But she was looking for someone specific. And there, second from the last, she was.

"Her," Sally said, pointing to one that went by the name of Amber, a brown-haired, blue-eyed woman, barely more than nineteen. She was a little shorter than Sally, and a little slighter too, with a bunch of freckles on her nose and cheeks, but if you had put them side-by-side, you might've sworn they were sisters.

"A fine choice," Ruby said. "Though you're all fine choices." She turned to Nox. "Are you sure you don't want one for yourself?"

"No."

"Two?"

"No."

"You can have the lot at a discount, if you want to make the most of it. One night and all."

Nox walked off.

"Suit yourself."

If Nox had suited himself, he wouldn't even be there. He'd be digging up Waltman, and burying someone else in his place.

Chapter Twenty

NOT EVERYONE WANTS
A SAVIOUR

Nox headed upstairs to his room, ignoring the
moans and screams of ecstasy from the closed
doors he passed. Then he heard a different kind of
scream, the shrill sound of pain. He halted, the echoes
of his footfalls drowned out by the cries of a woman,
and the sound of striking flesh.

"Move on," Sally told him.

When the woman screamed again, he could no
longer ignore it. He burst through the door, charging
in. Only his promise to Ruby made him keep his
guns sheathed, and it was a battle of wills to fight
the reflex of the draw. He hauled a large man off
the screaming woman, whose face was bruised and
bloodied, and soaked with tears. The man was taken
aback, surprised that anyone would dare interfere in
this sacred place of debauchery. He was even more
surprised that he was faced with someone who would
fight back.

It took a single well-aimed blow to the chin to
fell the man and leave him slumped on the floor. He'd
have to finish his fantasies in his dreams.

Nox extended a hand to the woman.

"What've you done?" she asked, recoiling from him. "Why did you do that?"

Nox hesitated. "I … was trying to save you."

Her bloodshot eyes widened. "Save me? Not everyone wants a saviour!" She got up, clutching the bedsheets around her naked body. "Oh God. Now he'll never pay!"

"But I thought—"

"You thought wrong! You've only gone and made a mess of things. Oh God. Ruby's gonna kill me." She paced around the room, letting the bedsheets inadvertently mop up some of the man's blood.

"I'm sorry," the Coilhunter said. "I was just trying to help."

"Well, don't!"

"I'll fix it with Ruby."

"Can you fix it with him?" she roared, pointing to the patron on the floor. "Just … just go!" She pushed Nox back out into the corridor and slammed the door, where he could still hear her sobs.

"I told you," Sally said. Amber said nothing.

Nox grumbled.

"Some of them like the pain," Sally added, gently slapping herself on the rear. "All of them like the money." She looked at Amber, who looked away.

"There are other ways to earn that," Nox said.

"What, like bounty huntin'?" Sally cocked her head. "Well, good night then."

Amber led her further upstairs, bringing her to a room on one end of the corridor. Nox went to his room on the other side. It had a comfortable bed, which he wasn't used to, but there was something about being in a place like this, where everyone had someone—even if they were bought—that made him feel incredibly lonely.

Sally locked the door in her room.

"Amber?" she asked. "Where'd you get that name?"

"Well, I couldn't really use my own, could I? Essa doesn't have the right ring to it here."

"Yeah, but … Amber?"

"Shut up. It's better than Handcart Sally."

Sally sauntered over to the bed and sat down beside Essa. "Sis, you've got to be careful here."

"I *am* careful," Essa protested.

"Not careful enough." Sally pulled the contraceptive amulet out of her pocket. She was almost surprised it was still intact, after everything she'd been through. She'd spent everything she had—or, more truthfully, everything she'd borrowed—to get it. She'd almost spent her life.

"You shouldn't have."

"I had to."

"How much did it cost?" Essa asked. She clenched her fists, refusing the jewel.

"Never mind the cost."

"I have to mind it. It'll get you killed!"

"Well, if you don't want a dune-belly, you better take this."

"But … Blood Johnson."

"Don't you worry 'bout him."

"I'm worried about *you*."

Sally shrugged. "It's too late now anyway."

"Don't say that."

"That's the Coilhunter out there."

Essa's face went pale. "C-c-can't you run?"

"I already tried. Tried runnin' from Blood too." She sunk her head and sighed. "I'm tired of it, sis. Tired of it all. I'd like to wake up one day and not feel like half the world wants my head."

They fell silent. Essa might have wanted to wake up one day and not feel like half the Ruby District wanted her body. Then again, she didn't seem as upset by the work as Sally was.

Essa took the amulet and put it around her neck. "I don't feel any different."

"Maybe that's a good thing. No demon buns bakin' away."

Essa forced a smile. "I'm happy here, Sally. You don't need to worry about me."

"I do. That's what big sisters are for."

Later that night, when Essa was sound asleep, Sally snuck out onto the communal balcony. The night air was chill and refreshing.

"Couldn't sleep, huh?" Nox asked her. He was resting, cross-legged, against the wall, staring up at the stars. There was a good view of them that night.

"I kept gettin' the feelin' there was a bounty hunter nearby," she said.

"Good intuition." He stared at her. "So it wasn't for you."

"Huh?"

"The amulet."

"So there *was* a bounty hunter nearby.

Eavesdroppin' an' all."

"You coulda told me you were doin' a good deed."

She laughed. "Would you have believed me?"

He gave the slightest shrug. "Probably not."

"Well then." She smirked at him. "Does that muddy that image you have of me?"

"A bit."

"Good."

They stared out at the night sky for a little longer.

"So, what's keepin' *you* up?" she asked.

"Same thing that always does."

"Crime?"

"Criminals."

She hung her arms over the balcony wall. For a moment, he thought maybe she was going to jump. "I don't think you'll ever get asleep then."

"Maybe not."

"You never answered me out in the desert."

"About what?"

"What made you."

He flicked the rim of his hat. "The Wild North made me."

"It made us all, criminals and everything."

"Guess I've gotta remake the desert then."

She turned back to him. "Y'know, you're always lookin' to save everyone." She shook her head, letting those golden waves quiver. "But who's gonna save you?"

Chapter Twenty-one

DEPARTURE

Nox didn't just spend the night staring at the stars. When Sally eventually went to bed, he headed downstairs to find the first of his supply crates already there. He had to hand it to Ruby. She was damn efficient. Then again, he was paying well above market price for these.

Nox pulled out some of the tools inside. They weren't quite as good as his own—after all, he'd made them himself—but they'd do the trick. Then he got to work repairing the various attachments on his arms, most especially the tracking device on his left wrist. It took him most of the night, or whatever was left of it, until he fell asleep against the crate.

He heard a sound like gunfire and stirred with a snap, pointing the pistols he'd been using as a pillow. Some found comfort in fluff and feathers, but the Coilhunter found it in cold, hard iron.

"You don't sleep easy, do ya?" Sally asked. She kicked the crate again. It didn't quite sound like gunfire now.

Nox grumbled and got to his feet. He put his guns away slowly. He was surprised to find the other supplies already lined up for him. One of the crates was just bullets. He didn't fancy playing childhood cowboy again when he needed to be the real thing.

"I think this is our sign that it's time to go," he said.

"No breakfast?"

"No rest for the wicked."

"Well, we've already rested. I wanna eat."

Nox grumbled again and followed Sally into the dining area. Some of the scantily-clad women were there again, this time serving food and drink. Ruby waved from her own table on the far end. They joined her, though in Nox's case quite reluctantly.

"Did you enjoy the night?" Ruby asked.

"It was better than the day, that's for sure," Sally said. She started into the food without asking, taking a big bite out of a chicken leg.

"I knew you'd like our Amber."

Sally smiled at Nox. "Sure did."

Ruby stared at the Coilhunter. "And you liked your supplies, I see." She turned back to Sally. "Amazing, huh? With everything on offer here, he gets off tightening bolts and fiddling with springs. Not the kind of screwing I'm into, but hey, whatever sieves your sand!"

Sally mumbled her agreement. She wolfed that food down like a starving animal.

"You not eatin'?" she asked Nox.

"I'll eat later."

"He's table-shy," Ruby said, "on account of the mask."

"Never thought of that," Sally replied mid-chomp. "Thought it was just for show."

"You've nothing to worry about here," Ruby told the Coilhunter. "No one gives two tosses what you look like, so long as you pay."

Nox stood up sharply. "You've got ten minutes," he told Sally. "I'll wait outside."

He walked off, leaving Sally to stuff her mouth even quicker. "He's a sensitive one," she mumbled. She stuffed a bread-roll in her pocket for the road.

Ruby nodded solemnly. "You have no idea."

When Sally had finished—or rather, when she'd spotted the Coilhunter pacing back and forth outside—she raced off, lifting her straw hat to Ruby. With all the people you could get involved with in the Wild North, she was glad her sister was under Ruby's wing, even if the job wasn't pretty. After all, it could've been Blood Johnson instead—and she was soon to be reminded of just how ugly that job of hers really was.

Nox had already gone through much of the supplies, whittling them down to the bare essentials. He had bullets strapped across his chest, and his belt was full. It seemed he'd tinkered with more of his toys while he was waiting.

"Right then," he said. "We go west."

"How are we gonna get out there? I hope you don't expect us to walk. Even Blood Johnson wasn't that cruel."

"I don't," Nox said. He pressed a button on his wrist. The monowheel pulled up beside him of its own accord.

"Coulda done with that yesterday."

Nox tapped his wrist. "If this hadn't been busted,

sure."

"So," she said, running her fingers along the rope strapped to the Coilhunter's belt. "You want me with or without the noose?"

"Without. If you were gonna run again, you woulda ran last night."

"Maybe I just wanted a good night's sleep first."

"You ain't helpin' your case."

She said no more. She was about to hop in the box in the back when she noticed the metal duck perched inside.

"Well, now I know where they got the name."

"What name?" Nox could think of a dozen they'd given him over the years.

"Mr. Wacky and Mr. Quacky."

Nox raised an eyebrow. "Who uses that?"

Sally shrugged. "I've heard it around. Mostly the kids."

Nox grumbled. "I prefer the other names."

"I think they have worse ones, y'know."

Nox started the monowheel up. "I'm sure they do."

Chapter Twenty-two

CAMPFIRE CHAT

They travelled for a long time, swiftly leaving the red glow of that desert haven behind them and entering under the harsher red glow of the sun again. It didn't quite beat them down as bad this time, but it kept on beating.

It was a long way still to the wastelands in the west. Sally dozed in the box at the back, her legs dangling over the edge, her head bobbing back and forward. She had the duck in her arms, clutching it almost like a bedtime bear. It reminded Nox of little Ambrose. He didn't like the reminder.

They didn't stop until the light got real low and the night frost set in. They huddled around a campfire, where Sally cooked some beans from the supply.

"You must be sidelappin'," she said.

He shrugged.

"Come on. I don't want you faintin' at the wheel." She handed him a bowl of beans.

He tried to stifle his sigh, then slowly began turning a bolt on the side of his mask. It swung open, revealing the blackened, disfigured skin beneath. He was glad it was night.

Sally didn't flinch like he thought she would, like

so many others did in the past. "How'd it happen?" She kept on eating. He was surprised it didn't ruin her appetite. Maybe nothing did.

"A fire," he said. He shovelled the beans in. He hadn't realised just how hungry he was. He also wanted to just get it over with so he could shut the mask again. He usually ate alone.

"What kinda fire?" she asked with a slurp.

"The one that burns."

She rolled her eyes.

"The one that killed my family."

"Ah."

"That's why we're chasin' Waltman's ghost."

"What if … he doesn't have the answer?"

He knew his stare was sinister with the campfire flickers. "You better hope he does."

They slept around the campfire, though the Coilhunter slept a little farther away from it than she did. He found it hard to drift off at first, but then exhaustion took him. It didn't take him anywhere pretty. It took him back to that night, back to the fire.

Chapter Twenty-three

BAD DREAMS

The fire started downstairs. Just a little flame, but it grew big fast, and spread throughout the house. It was nighttime when it happened, so the fire stood out starkly against the blackness, but it also caught them unaware. It caught them sleeping.

Nox saw it from a distance. The house blazing. His house. His family. Everything else faded into the blackness of the night. All that existed was the flames.

He sped along in the monowheel towards it, burning rubber, even burning his leg against the heated engine as he pushed it beyond its limits. He felt the burn more than ever, the taunting of the flames.

He arrived to screams. He leapt from the monowheel, letting it crash to the ground around him. He jumped and ran, straight towards the fire, towards the sealed doors, meant to stop intruders.

"Nathaniel!" his wife screamed from up above. He stood back until he could see her at the upstairs window, clutching his daughter Ambrose close to her. "Daddy!" the girl screamed. That scream was now seared into his mind.

The smoke gathered around them, strong and suffocating.

"Jump," Nox urged. It was a long drop. "I'll catch you."

Emma helped Ambrose up onto the window sill. Her nightgown billowed in the breeze.

"I can't," Ambrose said, her teeth chattering.

"You can, honey," Nox said. "Don't worry. I'll catch you."

Her feet teetered on the edge. For a moment, it almost looked like her mother was going to push her out. The flames were getting closer. The smoke was getting thicker.

Then there was a sound like a clap of thunder, and Ambrose fell. Nox was shaken by the sound, and it was luck or fate that ensured his arms were where they needed to be to catch the girl. He heard Emma scream above, but Ambrose was strangely silent. He looked down at her to see a patch of blood on her nightgown, near her stomach.

"What's this?" she asked faintly, mopping up some of the blood with her hand.

Nox turned. He could see nothing in the darkness all around. All he could see was the image of Ambrose in his mind.

"There's someone out there!" Emma shouted. He saw her pointing into the darkness.

Nox tried to set Ambrose down, but the girl clutched his arm. Her grip was very weak. "Why is this night darker?" she asked. Her hand fell limp.

Then there was another bang, and Emma tumbled from the window, landing with a thud on the ground below. Nox pulled his pistol out, holding it with his own blood-covered hands, with Ambrose's blood. He fired a single shot into the darkness, but he didn't know where he was shooting.

He knelt down to Emma, but she was already dead.

"Dad!" little Aaron shouted from the house. His voice was far off. He wasn't at that window.

Nox let go of Emma's quickly-cooling hand and raced around the outside of the house, keeping his pistol raised. He saw Aaron hanging halfway out another window, ready to let go and break his legs. Nox held out his arms to catch him.

The thunder came again. The glass of the window smashed from the bullet, and Aaron yelped. It missed him, but he crawled back inside, back to where the flames were waiting, to the safety of the smothering smoke.

Nox unloaded every bullet into the darkness around. "God damn you!" he roared.

There was no answer.

He looked back up to the window, but Aaron wasn't there.

"Aaron!" he shouted up.

The boy never came back.

Nox raced around the building, kicking in the nearest door. The fire was everywhere, just like the darkness outside was everywhere, just like the shooter seemed to be everywhere too.

Wisdom would have pushed him back outside, but love and desperation pushed him in. The flames danced their deadly dance, gnawing away at the wood, bobbing here and darting there. Inside the mouth of the house, the flames spat at him, catching the ends of his trouser legs, clutching the tips of his hair.

He bounded up the stairs, through the black smoke, coughing and choking, guided only by his intuitive knowledge of the building, of his home on the edge of Loggersridge, now turned into a horror. He tripped, banging his knee on the edge of a step. It almost sounded like the blast of a bullet. The pain of it only distracted from the growing pain of the fire.

He crawled out onto the upstairs landing, pulling himself along the bannister rails with one hand, holding his singed shirt over his mouth with the other. The smoke stung his eyes like phantom needles. It stung his lungs as well.

"Aaron!" he barked, his voice hoarse.

There was no answer.

He tried to stand up, but was overcome by dizziness. The smoke didn't just sting now—it stabbed. His vision was blurred and blackened. He almost didn't realise he was gasping for air.

He stumbled on towards the child's bedroom, collapsing against the wall and pushing himself back to his unsteady feet. He faltered at the doorway, then fell, barely able to brace himself against the impact.

His hand caught something that wasn't just the floor. It was another hand, a smaller hand. It felt tiny and tender in his. The fire hadn't gotten to it yet.

"Aaron," he whispered, reaching out for the boy. He clutched that little hand, but it didn't clutch back.

For a moment, he thought that this was it, that this was how it would end. His consciousness faded for a moment as the smoke gathered around them like guests at a funeral. Then the fire lapped at his feet, and the burn brought it all back, gave him new vigour, a new thirst for life.

He grabbed the boy's body, holding him close, ignoring the limp limbs and bobbing head. He let the fire lie to him and tell him that the child's body was still warm. He let the flames lick his own face, blistering the skin. He shielded the boy from it as much as he could, shielding him with his own body, feeling the flames so that Aaron wouldn't, fighting back the thought that maybe he couldn't feel at all.

He raced down the stairs, those crumbling steps, feeling the fire lash his legs, feeling the smoke crush his lungs. His knees almost buckled several times, and if it was just him, he might have let them buckle. He might have just given up and leapt into the void. But for now, he ran.

He came outside, feeling the fresh air for what seemed like the first time. The burns felt suddenly more severe. He dropped to the ground, still clutching Aaron in his arms.

He crawled away from the house, cradling the boy, then laying him down gently on the dusty earth. He buried the words that came to mind: From ashes to ashes, from dust to dust, from earth to earth.

It was always hard to wake little Aaron, that wild wanderer, who wandered in his dreams. He was a wistful child, who always had a faraway look in his eyes. His eyes were closed now. If they weren't, they might have had the most faraway look of all.

"Aaron," Nox said. He pressed his hands against the boy's chest, pumping it gently. There was no resistance, no gentle rise and fall, no little thumping of a heart.

"Aaron," he said more desperately. His throat was raw. His face was raw. His lungs were raw. Somewhere, deep down, his heart was raw too.

He tried everything, but nothing worked.

The boy never came back.

Nox wanted to cry, but the tears were all dried up in him. Everything was ashes now.

He looked out into the blackness of the night, trying to see the gunman, trying to find who did this. He knew it was no accident. The fire was meant to look like one, but the shooter stayed to make sure that no one escaped. Maybe Nox was meant to die too. He almost wished he did. The only thing that stopped that wish was this dark, burgeoning sense of anger, this overwhelming need for justice, for vengeance.

He stared into the blackness, wanting to scream at whoever stood in the shadows. He searched for them, but saw nothing. He swore a silent oath that he would hunt them, that he would chase them through the shadows, even into the fires of Hell itself. They would hear the clap of thunder on their heels, and feel the blast of lightning from his gun.

Nox awoke in a sweat, as if he had been too close to the fire. It was always that same, all too vivid, dream. But it wasn't just a dream. It was a memory, burned into his mind as much as his skin. The campfire had gone out, leaving him alone with the shadows, except for Sally, still sleeping, like little Aaron. As he sat there, reliving it all, he wished for the oblivion of dreamless nights. Sometimes he wished he never stirred again.

That was the thing about bad dreams in the Wild North. You still had them when you woke up.

Chapter Twenty-four

THE WALL OF THE WEST

Sally commented on the Coilhunter's silence the next morning, and his tossing and turning in the dust of the night. His silence continued for much of the journey that day, until they came to the Wall of the West, a series of steep plateaus that extended for miles. From a distance, they looked impenetrable. Up close, they could see the narrow gaps between the cliffs, forming a maze of channels through the wall.

"I don't usually come this way," Sally told him. "I go north first, then around. Heard you can get stuck in the cracks."

"This is a shortcut."

"You know what they say about shortcuts."

"Yes," he said. "Long journeys and dead ends."

"You said it."

He didn't travel this way himself, or at least not often. There was no reason to come out this far. This was the wild of the Wild North, and people still liked their creature comforts. You wouldn't get any of them out here, just the creatures. The towering walls offered great shelter from the sun, but they also offered shade to the desert wildlife. He'd seen some of them scurrying into the crevices on his travels. He'd crushed some of them beneath the monowheel too.

They drove straight towards that monstrous barrier, barely seeing the small channel between the rocks until they were right on top of it. The air was cool and refreshing there.

"Y'know, the Regime wanted to mine these rocks," Sally said.

"Did they?" Nox asked with disinterest. He hadn't much time for the Regime, or stories about them, and there were plenty of those. That war seemed far-off. There was a different battle between criminality and common decency right here in the Wild North.

"Lookin' for iron, I'd wager."

"Yeah."

"Thank God we're a bit too wild for 'em, eh?"

"Yeah," Nox said. "Or thank the Devil."

"Ain't that the Regime leader?"

"I thought you said it was Blood Johnson."

"Well," she said. "I've met a lot of devils." She didn't say anything else, but he took her silence to mean she thought one of them was him.

The initial journey was quick, but then they came to the weeds that tangled in the shadow and grabbed the treads of the monowheel as it passed. They grew fierce and thick there, climbing up the walls themselves. Nox had to stop now and then just to slice through some with his knives.

Then they entered a kind of mire, where the sand was damp. Far be it for them to curse the location of water, but they cursed it all the same, for the wheel stuck. They were forced to get out and push it.

"So much for a short cut," Sally moaned.

"It's still shorter."

They'd barely pushed the wheel halfway through the mire when Sally yelped. She kicked a scorpion away, but several more gathered around them. Nox fanned the hammer of his revolver and killed half a dozen of them with ease. The others scurried away.

"Don't you worry," he said. "Ain't nothin' to fear from those."

Then he felt a sudden chill as what little sun got in there was blotted out altogether. He could see a vast shadow on the ground, covering him entirely. He could also see Sally's pale face and wide eyes. He turned his head just a little, enough to see the giant pincer of a colossal scorpion.

Chapter Twenty-five

THE WILD OF
THE WILD NORTH

Nox ducked just in time as the pincer snapped at where his head had been. He dived forward, knocking Sally to the ground, and rolled until he faced the giant scorpion with both guns blazing. The creature roared, scurrying to the side, snapping and stabbing.

Sally crawled to her feet, and Nox ushered her back behind him. Then the scorpion stabbed its tail down towards them. He shoved Sally back again and sidestepped out of the way of the barb. He fired straight into one of the creature's eyes, which sent it back screaming.

But it wasn't alone.

Giant scorpions came from every channel in the granite walls, clapping their claws, dangling their bladed tails. One of them was larger than the rest, an albino scorpion with slightly translucent skin. Nox and Sally stood back to back, watching the creatures gather. They were surrounded.

"Take my shotgun," Nox said.

Sally reached behind her, her hand fumbling until it caught hold of the four-barrel shotgun that was strapped to his back. She pulled it out and cocked the barrel.

"You know how to use it, I hope," he said.

"Yeah," she replied with some hesitation.

"You've got four rounds." He flexed his fingers. "Make 'em count."

He dived, and fired as he fell. The nearest scorpion charged in, but took a bullet to the eye, shrieking and stabbing wildly. Nox heard the blast of the shotgun as Sally destroyed one of the claws of the pale scorpion. It howled, and its cry called the others to it.

Nox yanked a chain of bullets from his chest as he rolled. A few of them fell loose and he scrambled to get them, forcing them into the open barrel. He'd barely put them in when a scorpion reared up over him. He turned and blasted it, until the barrel was empty again. It screeched, then collapsed down on top of him, its right pincer twitching away.

Sally helped haul him out, but the distraction left her with her guard down. One of the scorpions snapped at her shotgun, pinning it in its claw. It pulled, tugging her towards it. Nox filled up the gun again, but the ammunition was getting low. He unloaded them at Sally's attacker, sending it back to the circling scorpions, which hemmed them in like a boxing ring.

The gun felt a lot lighter. One bullet left. He'd been keeping count. These were good enough for the normal scorpions of the Wild North, where just one bullet was enough, but they didn't seem to be doing much against their larger kin. He needed a bigger gun, and Sally wasn't going to give it back so easily.

She was also down to one shell.

They gathered again, back to back. The encircling enemies were fewer now, but that didn't matter if there wasn't enough ammunition to kill them.

"I hate to say it, but I think we need to run."

"Hell yeah," Sally said.

"You go cut us a path with your final round."

She aimed at the smallest of the scorpions, which was still one and a half times her height. The blast forced it back, tearing apart its shell. Nox dashed towards it, leaping onto its back. The stinger came down like a piston, but he kept on moving. Sally followed swiftly, and the duo slid down the side of the creature's back, barely touching the sand before they were off again. The last time they'd ran like this, he was hunting her. They never thought they'd be running together, and that something else would be the hunter.

They heard the thump of the scorpions' legs on the ground behind them, a flurry of noises as the creatures gave chase. They screeched and howled, and they snapped their claws menacingly. They kept their stingers raised, ready for the strike.

Nox and Sally ran, hand in hand, their other hands brandishing their now useless guns. They charged down narrow passages, turning sharply through the maze of channels, left and right, while they heard the never-ending scurrying behind them.

Then Nox felt a tug on his arm, and Sally's hand slipped through his fingers. He turned, ready to fight, ready to pull her back, but one of the giant scorpions already had her boot in its pincer claw. She screamed as she was dragged off, letting go of the empty shotgun, like she let go of his hand. He fired the last round from his gun, piercing the shell of one of the claws. The scorpion shrieked, but it didn't let go. It scurried away faster, pulling Sally with it, dragging her down the slope into its subterranean den.

Chapter Twenty-six

SNAPPERS AND STINGERS

Against his better judgement, Nox charged after the fleeing scorpion, until three more crowded in to shield it. He skidded to a halt before them, then turned and ran again, hearing the snap of shells a little too close to his ears.

He spotted a crevice in the wall to his left, which he threw himself into, clambering across the uneven rocks until he squeezed into a part the gigantic scorpions couldn't reach. Or so he thought. Even as he gave a sigh of relief, a stinger came through the crevice, piercing the ground right between his legs, a little too close for comfort. He gasped and kicked his legs, pushing himself back until the stabbing tail couldn't reach him.

Nox rested on his elbows and caught his breath. He shook his head and sighed, then turned to see a small scorpion perched on an outcrop near his head.

"What're you lookin' at?" he said. He took a deep breath and sent a puff of black smoke out of his mask, which scared the creature away. If only it were that easy for the rest of them.

He wasn't sure what to do. Guns didn't seem to work, and he didn't have much of them left anyway.

He doubted the toxins of his mechanical butterflies would have much effect. He was running out of options, and Sally was running out of time.

He got to his feet. The rock squeezed together tighter the further it went up. Both ends of the crevice were being watched by the giant scorpions, which periodically snapped their claws menacingly at him, or gnawed away at the rock on the edge. He needed a distraction.

Then it dawned on him.

He hammered his fist down on the tracking device on his left wrist. Elsewhere, still stuck in the mire, the monowheel's treads began to rotate, though it barely moved in the sludge. He could hear the engine hum even from here. He was sure the scorpions could hear it too. They raced away to investigate.

He leapt out, running for the den they'd pulled Sally into. He dived into the hole, tumbling down into a dark chamber full of eggs. The large scorpion was there, nudging Sally into the corner. It hadn't killed her. It hadn't even stung her yet. It was keeping her alive and warm, fresh food for the newborn scorpions that would soon hatch. Some of the eggs wobbled in place. It wouldn't be long now.

Sally looked at him with desperate eyes. The scorpion looked at him with angry ones.

He needed a distraction for this one too.

"Stay perfectly still," the Coilhunter told Sally.

He reached for his belt and tossed several orbs into the air. They burst open, and out of them swarmed his copper butterflies. The scorpion stabbed and snapped at them, but they moved quick. They sprayed it with toxins, but it had little effect. They went also for the bobbing eggs, and this drew the ire of the scorpion even more. It charged over to them, swiping and swatting, leaving room for Sally to escape.

She ran, but then some of the motion-tracking butterflies spotted her movement and flapped after her. Nox grabbed her hand and pulled her out of the den, before hitting a switch on his arm, which caused all the butterflies to fall dead to the ground.

Nox and Sally were back outside, but they weren't safe there either. More scorpions were gathering. This was a nesting ground. It'd soon be a feeding ground too.

They fled down new passages between the crowding cliffs, halting when the way was blocked by scorpions, turning sharply here, even sharper there. There seemed to be no end to the maze. They weren't trying to find the centre. They were trying to find the way out.

Nox kept battering the buttons on his arm. The thrum of the monowheel's engine was fading. It'd barely moved through the mire, and it was under strong attack by scorpions, who left many dents and scratches across the vehicle.

Many more of them charged after the fleeing duo. The number seemed to grow by the second. More came out of every passage they passed, until there were dozens of scorpions of all sizes bounding after them.

Nox looked up as he ran, searching for somewhere to fire his grappling hooks. The walls went up seemingly endlessly. There didn't appear to be much in the way of outcroppings and crevices to hook onto.

"Grab on," he told Sally, offering her his left hand. She held it tight.

He fired the grappling hook attached to his right arm. It rocketed up towards the sky, towards the high walls, but grasped nothing, then fell back down with a clang. He flicked his wrist to reset the mechanism, and the hook started to recoil into the launcher, while the scorpions tried to snap at the metal prongs.

He fired again, just as the attackers were closing in, and the hook caught on a small bit of rock that jutted out overhead. It hauled him upwards, and Sally came too. They dangled over the gathering horde, wondering if the scorpions would leave, worrying that maybe they would stay all day and night until food rained down from the sky.

Then the purr of the monowheel came, and the vehicle spun around the corner, crashing into the wall on the other side, before making straight for the crowd of scorpions. It cut through them, flattening some of the smaller ones, scaring away the larger. They broke apart, screaming.

Nox looked at Sally. "Run."

He let her go, and she tumbled on the ground. She chased the monowheel as it continued through the passage, clearing a path for them. Nox followed, yanking the hook free. As it snapped back, he swung it wildly, letting it clatter off a few of the smaller scorpions that dared to chase him.

They kept running, and he kept steering the monowheel with periodic directions entered on the controller on his wrist. In time, it found them a way out, and made the way clear with all its noise and fumes. They came out the other side of the Wall of the West, panting and wheezing. The monowheel grunted as it slowed to a halt.

"Bloody shortcut, huh?" Sally cried. She rested her hands on her knees, gasping.

Nox glanced back. The scorpions were retreating. "Well, it was shorter."

Sally leant against the wall, still trying to catch her breath. Nox inspected the monowheel. The paint was scratched bad, and there was sand and muck encased in the treads, but it was still in working order.

Then something set him on edge. He felt a sinking in his gut. He turned sharply to see a giant scorpion crawling down the wall above Sally. He reached for his guns, but they were empty.

He gave a cry, but it pounced on Sally. She fell on her back, kicking and screaming, waving her arms madly. Nox dived in, bashing at the creature's face. He pulled a dagger from his belt and stabbed it wildly, barely managing to evade its blows. It squirmed and shuddered, then collapsed to the ground.

Nox pulled Sally loose, but before he got her fully free, the giant scorpion raised its stinger over her, let it dangle for a moment, then dropped it fast. The sting pierced her like a blade, and she gave out a cry. The venom pumped inside her, even as the insect's heart stopped pumping altogether.

Nox yanked the stinger free, but it had already injected a lethal dose. He knew it instinctively, and from the look on Sally's face, she knew it too. The scorpion spasmed in place as Nox dragged Sally further away, resting her back against the monowheel.

"I guess it's … fate," she said, cringing.

The Coilhunter shook his head. To someone who had ended so many lives, fate was a gun. He opened a pouch on his belt and pulled out a vial.

"Take this," he said. "It'll slow the poison."

She held up the vial, looking at the odd-coloured liquid inside. "How much should I take?"

"The lot." He didn't have the heart to tell her that it likely wasn't enough. It was meant for smaller scorpions with smaller stings. By his guesswork, she'd be dead within a day.

She swamped the liquid down, and it had a noticeable effect. Her breathing became less fleeting, and some of the colour returned to her face. But the poison was still there, diluted a little, but working away nonetheless.

Nox paused for a moment. He was faced with a dilemma. He could try to bring her back to his hideout, where he had more anti-venom ready and waiting, but that was more than a day's ride. If she died on the way, he'd never find his answer. Or he could push on with her, and not tell her that each step was one closer to death. She'd die out there in the wastes, but at least then he had a chance to find out what Waltman knew, what he'd been chasing for all this time.

"So," she said, getting to her feet. She looked at him, as if she could read the struggle in his face. "Are you comin'?" She hopped forward, cringing from the pain. "I think this is gonna slow us down."

"Yeah," he said, regretting his shortcut more than ever. It'd slow them down all right. Death had a way of doing that.

Chapter Twenty-seven

NO COUNTRY
FOR LIVING MEN

After a brief inspection of the monowheel, and a quick restock of their weapons from the vehicle's spare supply, they set off again, slowed and wounded, but not altogether beaten. Nox heard Sally moaning periodically in the back. He could feel her body getting warmer. The fever was setting in.

The sun was falling fast asleep, but now they neared their destination. It was quite a thing to think of a place more desolate than the endless expanse of the Wild North, but there were pockets here and there where even the sun seemed to dare not tread, where the sands gave way to a cracked earth, barren even of the breeze. Here, under the great shadow of the wall of the vehicle graveyard that was the Rust Valley, was another resting place for unknown and unseen things, a territory unclaimed and unwanted, watched only by the empty eyes of the metal dead.

"We should walk the rest of the way," Sally suggested.

"Why?" Nox wondered if she'd even be able to walk.

"This monowheel'll draw the attention of them

clockwork constructs."

"Do they come out this far?"

"For scavengin', yeah."

"Fine," the Coilhunter said. He thought he could probably outrun those mechanical monsters if he kept his wheels, but then some of them had wheels too, or tank treads, ripped from vehicles they hauled into their iron web. He figured it'd be best to follow Sally's advice. After all, she knew these parts better than most.

He halted the vehicle and stepped off. Sally struggled off behind him, one knee buckling. She was evidently trying hard not to seem like she was weak. He was trying hard not to seem like he noticed.

"Now I know why you bring a wooden cart," he said, "and why you pull it manually."

"Yeah, I didn't do it out of love for manual labour, y'know."

He stared at the jagged mountains of scrap vehicles in the distance, hiding the setting sun. The Rust Valley was a mechanic's nightmare. It was where machines went to die—or to live as clockwork constructs under the watch of the Clockwork Commune.

"Would ya ever go there?" Sally asked him. She was making quite an effort to make small talk, maybe just to prove she could still do it. Her eyelids drooped down periodically, as if she was fighting off sleep.

Nox shook his head. "I'd never be caught dead there."

She forced a smile. "What about alive?"

* * *

139

They walked for what seemed like hours, feeling the shiver of the shadows as the sun abandoned them. That fiery eye wanted to kill you, but this land was no place for the living, so it turned its gaze elsewhere.

"Here," Sally said, stopping suddenly. How she knew the place was beyond the Coilhunter's reckoning. It looked the same here as anywhere in the wastelands, dark and empty.

"This is it?" he asked her.

"Around here." She stumbled in place, getting her footing again. "I think. I didn't really consider I'd be back to dig it up again."

"Yet here we are," Nox said, handing her a shovel. It was mostly for show, and for support.

She dug, and he dug. The earth crumbled apart at the slightest touch, like the bones of the long dead. Thankfully Waltman wasn't dead long enough for that, or his secrets might've died with him.

"There," Sally said. "I've got something."

They kept digging, until they unearthed Waltman's body. It looked like he'd gotten a blow to the head. It also looked like they'd decided to bury him before they were certain the blow had done the trick. One way or another, he was certainly dead now.

Sally reached down, pulling a rolled-up note from Waltman's grasp. It was odd how tightly he held it.

"They told me to bury the evidence too," she said. "I … I didn't read it. Thought it best not to. None o' my business and all."

"None of your business," the Coilhunter mused. "So says the gravedigger to the dead."

He snatched the paper from her and straightened it out. Nox could feel the blood leave his face.

"What's it say?" Sally asked. *Now* she was curious.

Nox couldn't quite get the words through the noose of his throat.

Sally grabbed the paper and held it up, bemused. "It's just symbols."

Nox knew those symbols. He and Waltman had come up with them some years ago, a kind of code. There were just two of them on the paper: a spiral and an arrow. Or the way he read it: a coil and a hunter.

It was hard to accept what the message said. If Waltman had a clue to who the killer was, and this was it, then it meant Nox was wrong to be looking for a criminal. He should have been looking for a bounty hunter. He should have been looking for someone just like him.

Chapter Twenty-eight

WHAT THE DEAD TELL US

Nox sat down, clutching the paper close, like maybe he'd hold the hand of his wife or the hands of his children. You could try to hold the hands of a ghost, but those spectral fingers would just keep on slipping through.

Waltman's dead eyes stared up, empty. The sky stared down, empty too. There were no stars that night. Just that black veil, that funeral pall.

The criminals hoped the dead were eternally silent. Many were. Sometimes, though, the ghosts of them stirred. They might not have had voices, but they spoke all the same. The Coilhunter had learned that well enough before, but some lessons kept on teaching.

He rifled through all the names and images of his fellow lawmakers, all those bent on bringing some frontier justice back—back from the dead. Some of them were good people, others not so much. He wasn't entirely sure where to start. He had an inkling though.

If you ever wanted to get a start in the business, there was probably no better place than the Deadmakers' Den. That said, if you were looking for law, order, and justice, there was probably no worse place. Oh, they spoke the words all right, but they didn't walk the walk. It was one thing to have a gunslinger's gait. It was quite another to have a lawman's soul. You'd go through a lot of bounty hunters trying to find one of those. Nox thought he might just have to go through them all.

The Coilhunter's attention was drawn back to Waltman's body, and those cold, dead eyes. What had he seen with them? Whose image was burned into the retinas? Some said there were Magi out there who could read stuff like that, the so-called soothsayers of the soul. Nox didn't go in much for that. If magic did exist out here, it didn't work anywhere near as good as lead in a barrel.

His thoughts focused on Waltman. He was a good man, as men go. Sent by the Regime to look after the Bounty Booth. He'd been there as long as the Coilhunter could remember, as long as he was hunting bounties. He'd been good to Nox, gave him some direction when he felt lost, gave him some easy kills when he was starting fresh. You always remembered your first kills. Nox remembered that he'd barely gotten his. He recalled how proud Waltman was. He was like a father to him. It seemed the Coilhunter just wasn't allowed to have family.

Sally seemed awfully quiet. He glanced at her, and she worked hard to form a smile. Her face was covered in sweat. It was too cold for that.

The Coilhunter rose.

"Right then," he said, looking at that little slip of paper that cost Waltman his life. "I guess I gotta hunt a bounty hunter."

Chapter Twenty-nine

WHAT THE LIVING DON'T

Sally fell suddenly very ill, fainting on the spot. He held her head up, tapping her gently on the cheek.

"You got any more of that syrup?" she asked, her voice weak.

"No."

"Pity."

"Yeah." It was a pity all right. It was more than that.

She tried to grab his hand, but couldn't find the energy. "I'm sorry, y'know."

"For what?"

"Buryin' 'im out here."

"Well, at least you dug him back up." He wiped her face with his neckerchief.

She coughed. Even that was weak. "I guess it really is fate."

"It's not," he said, knowing too well that, once again, fate was him.

"I hope you find him."

"So do I."

"I hope ..."

"Yes?"

She faded off, and he closed her eyes. Often he

just left them staring, but this time it seemed like she was staring into his soul, and seeing the rot there. He pressed his fingers at her throat. There was still a very faint pulse, but the poison would make short work of that.

He sighed, casting a glance at the grave where Waltman lay. It certainly did seem a little like fate that the last grave Handcart Sally had dug would inadvertently be her own. He gave it a moment, enough for a silent requiem, then rolled her body into the hole. She dropped down onto Waltman, hugging his cold body with her cooling one.

Poor Waltman, he thought. It was quickly followed by: *Poor Sally*. He didn't like thinking that, because that made it complicated. It was better when it was black and white. The good guys versus the bad guys. Simple. There wasn't anything simple in the Wild North.

"It may not be fate," he said, casting the first bit of dirt into the grave, "but it's fittin.'"

Chapter Thirty

SCAVENGER

The walk back to his vehicle was more sombre than before. He wasn't entirely sure why. It wasn't the first time he'd buried someone. It wasn't the first criminal who ended up dead under his watch. But Handcart Sally wasn't like most of them. She'd been caught up in things against her will, or so she said. Somehow, for some odd reason, he believed her.

He was so lost in his thoughts that he barely noticed the object sailing through the sky over the towering scrapyard heaps of Rust Valley. When he finally gave it his full attention, he realised just what it was: a makeshift copter, one of those flying machines from the madmen of tomorrow. That was fine, but it was what it was carrying, hooked by chains, that made his heart leap: it was his monowheel.

"Damn," he said.

He followed the route it was taking, starting into a trot, then a full-on run. It was hovering low, probably from the weight of its latest catch. Nox hadn't heard of the Clockwork Commune taking to the skies, but it wouldn't surprise him. It was only a matter of time before they weren't content with their little scrapyard community of man-hating machinery.

He got closer, and it seemed the pilot must have noticed, because the copter started to veer off in another direction, deeper into the wastelands. Nox panted and wheezed as he tried to keep up, but he knew he'd be panting and wheezing a lot more if he lost his mode of transport. The journey back to civilisation was long and hard. The journey to the afterlife was easy.

Then one of the copter's engines seemed to choke up, and two of the spinning propellers stopped. It dipped a little, but it didn't quite fall. It seemed to simply rotate around to where another set of propellers kicked into action. The pilot, who didn't look like a clockwork construct from the Coilhunter's vantage point, sat in a chair that rotated around inside, coming out at another globular window. The monowheel spun below, the chains clattering off the hull of the copter.

Nox gauged how close it was, then pointed his right arm towards the copter and fired the spring-loaded grappling hook. It hooked onto one of the chains and hauled him off the ground. Whoever was inside must have panicked, because just as Nox's boots landed on the top of his monowheel, another of the copter's engine's conked out. The vehicle dropped almost completely before the driver could start up another.

Nox grabbed one of the chains and tugged on it. The copter itself might have been cobbled together, but these chains were solid. The scavenger wasn't going to let go of its prize so easily. Nox swung about for a moment until he came near a small compartment beneath the box at the back of the monowheel. He punched the button on the side and it opened up to reveal many tools he often used to repair the vehicle, including a blowtorch. He fired it up, burning through one of the chains. The monowheel swung down, causing the copter to dip again. The engine groaned.

The monowheel was now further away from where Nox hung. He swung towards it, firing up the blowtorch as he came near. He did this several times until the second chain was cut, sending the vehicle down into the sand below.

Nox still hung from the remaining chain. He could have just let the grappling hook loose and reclaim his vehicle beneath him. But the thing about scavengers was that some of them scavenged from the living, and there was another name for those: thieves. It might've seemed like a free-for-all to some who lived in the Wild North, but he liked to remind them that it wasn't free for everyone.

He grabbed a hold of one of the unmoving propellers, then unlatched the grappling hook, letting it coil back into the launcher. He pulled himself up with one hand, feeling his muscles bulge from the weight, and tried to reach for the handle of the nearest door. There were many of them, just like there were many windows, but the handle was just out of reach.

Then he heard something that sounded like straining machinery, and he realised that the driver was trying to turn on the propeller he was holding onto. If he did, it would slice through his hand just as easily as he cut through the chains. It moved a little, seeming to catch on something.

Nox hauled up his weight as much as he could, stretching further. His fingers grazed the handle, but that wasn't enough. Then he heard the chug of engineering, and he let go of the propeller not even a full second before it spun into action. He fired the grappling hook again, towards the door handle, where it pulled him up past the spinning blades of the propeller, but left him dangling a little too close. He had to pull his legs up to keep his feet out of the rotating metal.

He pulled himself up further until he could grasp the handle with his left hand, pulling the door open. He swung out with it, back and forward. Then he leapt towards the open doorway, barely grabbing the edge. He climbed inside, immediately getting to his feet. The inside of the vehicle was as ramshackle as the outside, with bits and pieces of machinery lying around the place, some attached with netting to the walls to help keep them in place when it rotated.

Nox kicked open the nearest door, making his way past one of the globular windows. He forced open another door, spotting the driver in his seat with his back to him in a large chamber.

Nox took out a revolver and pointed it. "Did your mother never teach you not to take what isn't yours?"

The driver spun around, revealing the oddest dressed man Nox had seen in a while, like someone from a carnival. He was decked out in high-heeled spotted boots, with a long multi-coloured fur coat over a frilly shirt and tight polka-dot trousers. His golden curls crawled out from a large hat of feathers and flowers.

"Oh!" he cried, when he saw the gun. "My mother taught me to scavenge. It's how we made our way."

"I'm bettin' she didn't teach you to steal."

"Oh, dear, no, pickle! If I'd known it was yours, I wouldn't have taken it!"

"Then why'd you keep on runnin'?"

"Well … you're kind of scary."

Nox smiled beneath his mask. "Yeah," he said, cocking the barrel. "I kinda am."

Chapter Thirty-one

THE ANTIDOTE TO THIEVERY

Nox fired, but even as he hit the trigger, the eccentric trader yanked the lever on his chair. The seat dropped, rolling down on a track until it came up again at the other side of the vessel, looking out at another globular window. Nox turned, aiming again, but he saved the bullet, because he could see the trader itching to hit the lever again.

"Please!" the trader shrieked. "I can explain."

"Explain it to God."

Nox made a feint, watching as the thief plummeted again in his odd pilot's chair. Few evaded the Coilhunter so easily, but he didn't so much as dodge as let gravity dodge for him.

Nox heard the chug of the wheels on the rails as the chair sailed beneath the metal grail he stood on. He quickly followed the sound, turning sharply onto another rampart that crossed over the other, charging up to yet another window.

He leapt, even before the trader emerged again. When he did, Nox caught hold of the chair and pulled himself up, much to the shock and terror of the thief. He grabbed the man's throat with his right hand, and when the trader made a motion to press the lever again, Nox drew his pistol with his left hand and pointed it at the man's hand.

"You know what the antidote to thievery is," Nox crooned.

The trader made a series of unintelligible cries and gurgles as Nox tightened the grip around his throat. His hat blew off in the next puff of smoke from Nox's mask.

"Spare me!" he pleaded. "I'll give you anything! Oh, spare me, please!"

"There's nothin' in this heap of junk I want," the Coilhunter replied, taking his hand off the man's throat to gesture around. As he did, he saw all the random pipework, the mismatching grails, the netting full of random objects, and several crates of medical supplies. He paused.

"Those," he said. "Do they have antivenom?"

The trader seemed surprised. "Uh … of course, love! This is the Wild North, after all!"

Nox sheathed his gun and leapt over to the crates. He dragged them down and opened all of them, pulling out the vials of antivenom and strapping them to his belt. It was more than he had at home.

"I don't want to know where you got these."

"Genuine business, plum, I promise!"

Nox scoffed. "I'm sure."

He prepared to leave, then spotted what looked like a special multi-purpose tool he'd devised to speed up repair work on vehicles, one that went missing from his workshop over a year ago. He tossed it in his hand and eyed the trader, who said nothing.

"You should join the Clockwork Commune,"

Nox said. "You'd be right at home."

"Why, I haven't got a home. Always moving."

"Always runnin', more like. I never got your name. Just in case I see it on a poster some time."

The trader hesitated. "Porridge. I never got yours."

"I'm just a man with a mission."

He kicked open the door and leapt down into the sand, tumbling down a dune. The copter veered off, and the Coilhunter reclaimed his stolen vehicle, giving it a once-over for damage. It was mostly cosmetic. He was lucky it didn't end up as part of the trader's vessel, or as another brick in the scrapyard walls of Rust Valley.

He fired up the monowheel and sped off, back into the wastelands that he had walked before. He pushed the vessel to its limits, knowing he didn't have that much time. He'd already lost too much.

He arrived at the patch of land where the unmarked grave was still noticeably fresh. He dug with a frenzy, exposing Handcart Sally's poor face. She often had a bit of soot on it from the mines, but now she had the soot of the grave. He pulled her out, jabbing her with the first vial of antivenom before she was even fully out. He tried another, and a third, before he even waited to see if they had any effect. The scorpion venom was slow, but he'd been slow to come back too. There was an antidote to the sting, but there was no antidote to death.

"Come on," he whispered, gently tapping her face. She seemed quite peaceful. Maybe he wasn't doing her much of a mercy at all by trying to bring her back. Everyone wanted to live forever, but not in Hell, and to many the Wild North was just that. It even had the red sands.

He felt for a pulse, pulling off his glove to get a better sense. If it was there, it was weaker than his coarse fingertips could pick up. He tried another two vials. He didn't want to overdo it, or the antivenom would become a poison of its own.

To his shock, she stirred.

He gave her some water from his canister. She opened her eyes and gave a gentle moan. She seemed groggy. Nox supposed the sleep of death was a bit harder to wake from. If only it was this easy to wake everyone.

"What happened?" she asked.

"You were tellin' me about your hopes."

She blinked.

"You didn't quite finish what you were sayin'." He shrugged. "I had to bring you back to hear the rest. You could say I'm a sucker for knowin' how it all ends."

She gave a faint smile. "I'm glad it didn't end like this."

But Nox didn't smile, and he was sure she saw it in his eyes. He didn't say anything, but his thoughts rang out loud and clear: *Don't be too happy. It might end worse.*

Chapter Thirty-two

WORKSHOP

They left the wastelands, a little happier and more relieved than when they entered, but Waltman's revelation played on the Coilhunter's mind as they travelled. He cycled through the list of bounty hunters he knew. Some of them were dead. He hoped this one, the killer of his family, was still alive, so that he could kill him himself.

He drove through the yellow sands, where the sun reared its ugly eye again, and into the red ones, while the sun began to fade. Sally was still weak and groggy. She moaned periodically, especially when the sun tried to finish her off. Nox had to stop twice to make small repairs to the monowheel and refill the tank with the two diesel cans strapped to either side of the box.

In time, they arrived at the Canyon Crescent, though by now it was so black that he had to guide the vehicle with the faint front lights, and a bit of muscle memory, and a dash of intuition. The cold came out to hug their once roasting bodies, forcing them to sit a little closer to the vehicle's engine. Sally wrapped her arms around Nox for warmth and faded off into a restless slumber, where she shivered every so often. He wasn't sure if it was from the cold or from whatever venom was still in her veins.

He followed the winding paths of the canyon, down slopes, around sharp bends. The red walls flew by in a haze, seen only in a fleeting glance of the headlights. The monowheel tilted here and there, turning down narrow channels in the rockface, until finally he slowed to a halt in a cavern that was barricaded up with large metal doors.

Sally stirred, blinking sleepily and murmuring to herself. It reminded Nox of how little Aaron used to wake. He was such a dreamer, it took him a long time to come back to the real world, with its cactus pricks ready to burst all hopes and dreams. Maybe in Sally's sleep, she dreamt the world wasn't withered, that she wasn't indebted to a ganglord, that her sister wasn't making a living in a whorehouse. Nox never dreamed like that. He only ever seemed to have nightmares.

"Where are we?" Sally asked, climbing off the monowheel. She almost faltered.

"Home," Nox said, pulling open some of the latches on the door. "Of a sort."

The great door creaked open, revealing a network of chambers etched into the rock, all man-made and reinforced with metal. Sally was used to mines, but nothing like this. It was a colossal workshop, filled with machinery, with tools carefully organised on the walls, and shelves full of little toy contraptions.

"Wow," she said. "You live here?"

Nox ushered Sally in, then went back for the monowheel. He parked it inside and closed the door behind. For a moment, everything went black. Then a motor kicked in and a series of lights came on, lining the top of the walls.

"Is that … electricity?" Sally asked.

"Yes."

"I've never seen it up close before. Well, at a fair once, but I thought maybe it was a trick."

"Everything's a trick, of sorts."

"How do you make it?"

"I have windmills up on the top of the cliff. When we get sandstorms, they generate enough electricity for a month. I haven't figured out how to use it in vehicles yet, not in a reliable way anyhow."

"Amazin'."

"I suppose."

"It is. Really."

Sally approached a series of shelves lined with toys. There was even a little metal windmill, which must have been like the ones perched on the cliff above. She reached towards them, but the Coilhunter charged in swiftly, swatting her hand away.

"Don't," he barked.

"Why? What's wrong?"

"Just don't."

"I've never seen anything like these. Did you make 'em?"

Nox turned away, walking further into the next cavern. He said nothing.

"Nox?" she called after him. She followed him into the next room, where there was a kind of landship, heavily modified. It looked incomplete. Parts and tools were scattered around it.

Nox continued through the next door.

"Why won't you tell me about your toys?" she probed.

He stopped. "Because those don't matter now. Not for this." He continued on, revealing another room, lined wall to wall with weapons. "These are the ones that matter now."

Chapter Thirty-three

PREPARATION

The Coilhunter barely rested that night. He toiled on his weapons and gadgets, taking two machine guns meant for his as-yet-unfinished landship and attaching them to the monowheel instead. Nothing quite beat that beast for speed. He thought that now that he was getting close to the prey, he'd need speed the most.

"How're you gonna find 'im?" Sally asked. She was feeling a lot better now, and looked it too. It seemed a good snooze in a grave did some people a world of good. For others, for the criminals, it just did the world good.

"I have my ways."

"So you do."

"There's the Deadmakers for a start."

"Oh," she said. "Them."

"One of 'em is bound to know something."

"Why?"

"That's the who's who of the bounty huntin' world. Anyone who's anyone'll be there."

"Why aren't you?"

"'Cause I don't wanna be. They invited me, but I turned 'em down. They're in it for the wrong reasons.

I don't wanna be in a killer's club."

"No," she said. "You wanna be alone."

He said nothing.

"Is this you?" she asked, holding up a newspaper clipping. It showed a black and white photograph of him with his wife and kids, labelled: *Nathaniel Osley Xander and his loving family*. Those were the kind of words that could've been etched on a tombstone. They might still.

He snatched the paper from her and put it away. He fought the urge to carry it with him. He thought maybe it might get rumpled or ripped. It was the only picture of them all together. He remembered the day well, when he was being celebrated as the local jack-of-all-trades for Loggersridge, having helped turn the town into a mechanical wonder, with its own steam-powered train, and lots of miniature ones for the children. He gulped down the thought and wiped the memory away with a tear.

He waited until Sally was well on the mend, giving it the better part of the next day. Otherwise, he would have already been off. He was itching to go, just like his fingers were itching to hit the triggers. He locked up his workshop and dropped Sally off outside the Burg, giving her a bag of coils to tide her over.

"What about Blood Johnson?" she asked.

"Don't you worry about him."

"I might have to. What if you don't come back from your little huntin' party?"

"Don't you worry about me."

"Not to seem selfish or anything, but I'm kinda

worried about myself."

Given everything they'd been through, and the fact she was still standing, he wasn't that concerned. Fate'd taken a shine to her. "I think you'll do just fine."

"Well, I guess this is goodbye."

He revved the engine. "I guess it is."

"My hopes," she said, pausing.

"What's that?"

"Before … y'know. I was gonna say somethin'."

"Yes."

"I hope you don't just find that killer. I hope you find some peace."

He tipped his hat to her, then pressed hard on the accelerator. For now, all he wanted was the killer. He thought maybe to find peace, he'd have to fight a war.

Chapter Thirty-four

THE DEADMAKERS' DEN

The Deadmakers' Den didn't have a location. It travelled around the Wild North, so no one except the Deadmakers themselves knew where it was supposed to be. It crawled across the desert on gigantic metal treads, travelling under the veil of night, acting as a hideaway for the elite bounty hunters during the day. It was a place of outcasts, and yet the Coilhunter was an outcast even to them. Though he'd been invited to join their exclusive club, where they would share tales of prized bounties, and sometimes contribute human trophies to the Den's Museum of Kills, he shunned them, finding no glory in the job, just duty.

Danny Deadmaker himself was there that night, lounging back in his great sofa, pipe in hand, gin in the other. He was adorned in black from head to toe, a little like a priest's attire, which gave rise to the idea that he was there to administer anyone's last rites. A priest might have done it with a holy book, but Danny Deadmaker did it with a pistol and a grin. His beard and moustache were as black as his clothes, and maybe his soul was blacker still.

Then there was Long-eyed Lizzy, with her

163

augmented eyepiece, permanently attached to her skull. They said she could see a mile away with that, though Nox had his doubts. What he couldn't deny though was that she could see farther than him. She was the go-to bounty hunter for a quiet kill. By the time the victim fell, she was already long gone. She often came back to the Den to boast about the latest distance. She always seemed to be in competition, but only with herself. No matter where she went, or who she was chasing, she always wore a dress. "A gal can be a killer and still be pretty," she often said. There was nothing like saying it with a skirt and a gun.

Then there was TNT Tom, Danny's father and the oldest of the Den-goers at close to a hundred. Somehow he'd escaped death, though the sun left many scars in the wrinkles of his skin. He hadn't let many escape himself, so sometimes they called him the Flycatcher. He could barely walk now, but this was probably due more to the crates of explosives he carried around with him. His art wasn't in the draw of the gun, but in luring his target into a trap. They usually couldn't walk after that either.

Then there was Iron Ike, a clockwork construct made to resemble, for the most part, a man. He was made of iron pipes and pistons, with copper rivets holding it all in place. No one was quite sure who made him, or if he wasn't really just a spy for the Clockwork Commune, but he worked like the rest of them, hunting the wanted, killing the marked, and when he was here in the Den, he rested and played like the rest of them too. For a place of outcasts and oddballs, he really did fit in.

Then there was Gold-barrel Jane, with her ponytail of auburn hair, tight trousers, and antique Treasury-forged gun. It was so old, it often jammed, but it was her signature piece, and she made it work more often than not. She was the newbie of the group, finding her way amongst the lawmakers of a lawless land. There were rumours she was the daughter of a Treasury duke, that this was her little rebellion. Some came to the Wild North to hide, others to make a dirty fortune, but some came to feel alive. It was always when you were close to death that you felt it most.

Then there was the Coilhunter, standing at the door, hands hovering over his revolvers, ready to draw, even more ready to shoot. It was almost as if he had just appeared there, and so it might have seemed to even the other bounty hunters, for he came in a haze of smoke, which was like the prelude of a smoking gun.

"Nox," Danny Deadmaker said, surprised. He sat up, attentive. He wasn't used to that, not in here. This was a place where you didn't have to look over your shoulder, but not tonight. "What brings you here?"

The Coilhunter's eyes were cold, even colder than theirs. The black smoke exploded out of the vent of his mask like that smoke that hung over a funeral pyre. He looked at them each in turn, one by one, marking them off on a list, drawing their faces on the posters of his mind.

"Waltman sent me."

"Waltman's dead," Long-eyed Lizzy said. For all her augmentation, she didn't see him coming.

"I know," Nox replied, "and one o' you is gonna join 'im."

Chapter Thirty-five

THAT DANGEROUS DRAW

There's nothing more dangerous than drawing a gun on a bounty hunter. That was something many criminals learned the hard way. It was quite something then when Nox drew both revolvers on the crowded room, and they, just as quick, drew theirs.

"Now, Nox," Danny said, nervous. His own pistol wasn't quite as steady as it should have been. He'd blame the drink, of course, but neck oil didn't make his fingers slip.

"What is this about?" Iron Ike asked in his usual dull, monotonous tone. He pointed a shotgun in the Coilhunter's direction, without a hint of unsteadiness.

Nox had one gun pointed at Danny and the other roaming from target to target. Each of them in turn reacted as it got to them, cocking their own guns, pointing them more forcefully.

"You know what it's about," Nox said. "Or at least *you* should, Danny."

Danny Deadmaker sat up. "Why me?"

"Why not?" Nox moved his roaming hand to his coat pocket, slowly. Any sudden movements could set off all those trained trigger fingers. He used one finger to pull out the slip of paper that contained

Waltman's code and flicked it into the centre of the room. It swung in the air like a feather, landing face up.

"I don't get it," Danny said.

"You know that code as good as I do."

"Sure. Is that not code for you?"

"Or you. Or her. Or him. Or all of you together." The travelling gun bobbed from one to another. The bullets almost begged for release.

Danny still seemed confused, so Nox made it nice and simple for him. "Waltman found out that the killer was a bounty hunter."

"The killer?"

"Of my family!" Nox roared.

The guns trembled. They knew how close he was to firing. They knew that even with a dozen guns pointed at him, he could take out a dozen of them before his body hit the ground. There were score charts in the Den, and some of them had the Coilhunter at the top, even though he wasn't a member. He was the one to beat. They never thought that maybe he was the one to kill.

"One of us?" Gold-barrel Jane asked. It likely wasn't her. She was too young, too fresh, too new to the game. She was also late to draw. She'd learn soon enough you couldn't do that too many times.

"Steady now, Nox," Danny said. "I'm sure we can sort this out."

"We'll sort it with lead. You know that well."

He did. They all did. There was no wondering about that. They only wondered which of them, if any, would leave the Deadmakers' Den tonight.

Maybe some of them would limp. Maybe some of them would crawl. Those would be the lucky ones.

"It wasn't us," Danny said.

"Maybe it was and maybe it wasn't. But there aren't many bounty hunters who don't come through these doors and don't sit at that bar. You know 'em all. You must've heard the tales. Someone knows something. Someone's gotta spill the beans or we'll be spillin' bullets soon, and spillin' blood."

"This isn't like you, Nox," Long-eyed Lizzy said. "You can't just shoot up the place."

"You'd be surprised what people can do. Like kill someone's family when there weren't no bounty on 'em. What you wouldn't be surprised by is that justice needs to be paid."

"This won't end good," Danny said.

"No," Nox replied. "No, it won't. But it'll end. Either people start talkin' or people start screamin'. You know the drill, and you know I mean it. Right now there's a bounty on all o' you. That's what Waltman's paper is, your little poster with no face and no name. Help me narrow it down. Give me a face for these bullets. Give me a name to bury."

Someone stirred in the corner. It was TNT Tom.

"You won't like what you find, Nox," he said.

Nox didn't like him. He always felt like he was scheming, like he saw the Coilhunter as just another fly.

"Maybe not, but I don't like not finding it either."

"Come with me then." Tom stood up, resting on his walking stick. When everyone else was trying not to move, he was the only one who ignored the barrels. He was fearless. You had to be to work with explosives. He'd been gambling with his life for decades, and so far he kept on winning.

The Coilhunter followed him through into the back room behind the bar, the place where other gambling was done. There was no one there tonight though. This was a night off, a night for drinking, a night for dying.

The others breathed a sigh of relief when the Coilhunter left. They lowered their guns and raised their glasses.

Long-eyed Lizzy strolled over to Danny Dead-maker and helped him up off his seat. "You better run," she whispered to him. "It's only a matter of time before he finds out."

Chapter Thirty-six

TNT

"Take a seat," Tom said.
"I'll stand."
"Come on, Nate. We're old friends, us."
Nox raised an eyebrow. "Are we?"
"Of course. We go way back."
"Back to when my family was alive."
Tom scrunched up his mouth. "Yes."
Nox pulled out a chair noisily, letting the screeches tear through Tom's old ears. He sat down, staring at Tom from beneath the brim of his hat, keeping one hand—and one gun—on the table, and the other reaching down to the ground. Sometimes you wanted a gun on show. Other times, you wanted it perched beneath the table.
Tom sat slowly, his legs almost buckling. He groaned audibly.
"You're gettin' on," Nox said.
"We're *all* getting on, Nate."
Nox's breath was heavy. "Not all o' us."
"Look, Nate. This hunt of yours, it's not good for you."
"It ain't good for whoever I'm huntin'."
"But you might never know."

Nox drew closer, resting both wrists on the table, keeping the guns pointed at Tom. "It got to the point that I thought maybe that was true. The trail was always pretty cool, but it kept on gettin' cooler. I'd resigned myself to maybe never knowin'. But now … the list has narrowed down a lot. There's maybe a hundred bounty hunters in the Wild North."

"Living ones," Tom said.

"There'll be less of those soon enough."

"Yes."

"Maybe just me and you. Maybe just me."

"Indeed."

"So, Tom," Nox said, taking off his hat and placing it down on the table. It revealed the scars along his head. The hair was cut tight around them. "Tell me what you know."

"All right, Nate. Do you remember when you and Dan were kids?"

"Like yesterday."

"A lot of yesterdays ago. Back in the good old days."

"When the sun didn't shine."

"Well," Tom said. "You and Dan never did get along, did you?"

"Boys'll be boys."

"And then you were men." Tom seemed suddenly agitated now. "And you were married, and my Dan was out in the cold. Emma was meant for him, you know."

"I don't get ya," Nox said. "She fell in love with me."

"She made the wrong choice, and you made the

wrong choice too. You shoulda backed away. You knew Dan had set his eyes on her."

Nox shook his head.

"I don't like seeing my boy disappointed."

Nox started to stand up, but he felt something holding him down. Metal cuffs sprang from the armrests of the chair and latched into place.

"What's this?" he asked.

"You're not the only one with gadgets, Nate."

Nox struggled, but the bonds were tight.

"Well," Tom said, hobbling to the door. He tapped his walking stick against a barrel of TNT there. "I guess you can have Emma after all. Till death do you part."

Back in the bar, the Den-goers were surprised to see TNT Tom waddle out. It wasn't often you went into a room alone with the Coilhunter and came out in one piece.

"The Den's closed," he said. "For refurbishment."

They didn't quite get what he meant until they heard the sizzle of a fuse in the back room. With TNT Tom, you didn't have to guess what that was. The bounty hunters charged for the door.

The explosion rocked the building, blowing a hole in the back. Some of them stopped at the door, but Tom kept on going, and Danny was already long gone. The rest of them stared at the haze of smoke and splinters, wondering if they should go straight to the scoreboards and wipe clean the Coilhunter's name.

Not yet.

He came out of the smoke, like he often did. He held one of his signature tools in one hand and an unclasped metal cuff in the other. His coat sparked with embers, and his eyes flickered with anger.

Chapter Thirty-seven

A WHOLE LOT OF HOGS

The other bounty hunters parted as the Coilhunter came through, kicking open the Den's door and stepping outside. He was greeted by a fleet of motorbikes, big and black, with thick wheels designed to cope with the uneven sands. On them sat rough bikers, decked to the nines with leather and studs. Emblazoned on the back of their coats, and the side of their bikes, was a flaming skull. Unsurprisingly, they were the Flaming Skull gang.

"Coilhunter," their leader, Ember, said.

Nox stepped down. They blocked the way entirely.

"Get outta my way," Nox said through his gritted teeth. The sound echoed in his mask.

"No can do," Ember replied. "We were hired with a job to do, and we're doin' it."

Nox eyed them one by one. They puffed their chests and revved their engines in response, but he didn't need any big gestures to seem menacing.

"I wanna fight," Nox said, "but not with you."

The Flaming Skulls were one of the "good" gangs, if there was any such thing. They were on the side of the law, for the most part, standing up for the weak. They had a code of honour, even if it was a bit of a bent code. They co-operated with the Deadmakers, passing on information, showing up in force when force was needed. Like now.

"Danny Deadmaker said you went and gone mad."

Nox shook his head. "Not yet. There's still time for that."

"Said you went and threatened his life."

"It wasn't just a threat."

"He's a good man, that Danny. Looked out for many of us. I thought you were one too, Coilhunter."

"He killed my family." Nox pointed his finger to the ground, to maybe six feet under. "There needs to be justice."

"Well, I don't know anything about that, but it doesn't sound like good ol' Danny."

"He didn't get a title like Deadmaker for no reason."

"And you didn't get one like Coilhunter for none either."

Nox sighed. "You don't know what you're doin', Ember. You don't know how close to the fire you are. Get outta my way and you won't get burned."

"As I said, no can do. Danny's been good to us."

"Don't make me be bad to ya."

"Stand down, Nate."

"I don't go by that name any more. That man died when my family died. I buried him as well. But there's still space inside that grave, space for the killer. I'm askin' ya one more time: get outta my way."

"I guess it's a stalemate."

The door creaked open behind them and out

came Iron Ike, who halted with a clang. "Oh," he said. "I thought this would have been finished by now. You humans take an awful long time to get things done."

"Ain't that the truth," Nox said.

He charged at Ember, who was caught by surprise, then threw himself over the end of the bike, tumbling in the sand. He raced to his monowheel and dived into the driver's seat. He was lucky it was a biker gang that tried to stop him, as they knew not to touch another man's wheels, even more than touching another man's wife. That was part of the code for all of them, no matter how criminal they were. It wasn't just the code that stopped them though: it was the duck, perched in the box at the back.

He sped off, but the bikers had him circled. He drove towards one, but the biker didn't baulk, and the Coilhunter didn't feel like crashing. He turned sharply, sending sand up into the face of the biker. He tried another route, but it was blocked as well. They weren't there to fight him, but they weren't going to let him escape.

So he took the only route he could, straight into the Deadmakers' Den, and out the blasted back, firing the new machine guns to cut a bigger door. The bikers had already started to gather there, but they hadn't quite ringed him off. He drove up a dune, flying over the head of one of the bikers and sending up a plume of dust behind him.

Now he was in the wide expanse, and the sun was quickly setting. He knew he had to be quick or the trail would vanish into the obscurity of the night. By morning, those tracks left by Danny Deadmaker and

TNT Tom would be gone. He only hoped the Flaming Skulls hadn't messed them up too much already.

He heard their engines revving behind him, drowned out only by the purring of his own. He hammered his elbow down on a latch at the side, and out of the back of the monowheel came a hundred little balls, encrusted with nails. The bikers swerved, but a few of them drove straight through, suffering punctured wheels as a result.

Ember pulled up beside him. Each of them fell back a little in turn, until they matched each other's pace.

"This is madness," the biker shouted against the wind. His hair flailed madly behind him.

Nox kept his eyes on the tracks ahead.

Ember pointed a pistol at him, but Nox knew he wouldn't fire. No Flaming Skull would shoot a man on his machine, and certainly not a man who didn't do wrong. That ruled out a lot of people in the Wild North, but it didn't rule out him.

"I made a promise not to shoot you," Ember shouted.

Nox drew the shotgun from the side of the monowheel and pointed it at the biker. "I made no such promises," he rasped, then shot the back wheel instead. The motorbike careened off as Ember lost control, skidding into the sand.

The incident meant Nox didn't see the bike drawing up on the other side, and the biker stretching across a long bar with a hook on the end. He grabbed a hold of one of the metal tubes of the engine, pulling himself closer.

Nox grabbed the bar and tried to reef it free, but it held on tight. The biker reached out to him, grabbing his arm. Nox rolled his shoulder to loosen the grip, but it held on just as tightly. So Nox turned the monowheel sharply, tearing the biker from his bike. The man clutched the end of the bar for a moment, bashing off the sands, until he rolled off down a dune, leaving the hooked bar behind him.

Nox unhooked the bar and tossed it behind him, where he heard it smack off the head of one of the bikers behind. That unconscious biker then drove into the next one beside him, and both of them veered off into a heap at the side.

The Coilhunter continued on, but the biker gang started to fall behind. He wasn't sure why they were giving up so easily, but then he saw it. The wind was working the sand up into a frenzy ahead. A storm was brewing, and not just in the Coilhunter's head.

Chapter Thirty-eight

SANDSTORM

It started as a gentle haze, like a summer shower, if it ever rained. Then the winds kicked up a frenzy, and the further he pushed on, the more they pushed back. He squinted his eyes as the grit came like little boulders, pelting off his mask. He had to tilt his hat down until he secured his goggles on, but soon they started to clog up too, until he found himself in the howling sandstorm, barely able to see anything in front of him.

No, he told himself. Maybe he was speaking to the gods, or whoever worked this weather like loyal machinery. He scoured the ground, but he couldn't see it clearly enough. The tracks were already shifting. The storm was growing. The sands were thickening.

Then he spotted something black in the haze, something small, something that was then just as quickly shrouded in sand again. He swerved, realising just in time that it was a mine. Then he saw another, and turned again. The dunes were littered with them, freshly dropped. He knew who had put them there. For the first time ever, he knew. They didn't care if the Flaming Skulls drove into them too. They didn't care who died, so long as it wasn't them. They thought

180

it would stop or slow him, and maybe it would, but with the tracks swiftly fading, these were the new iron breadcrumbs, leading the deadly way.

He had to push the vehicle harder, fighting against the fierceness of the wind. Normally when there was a sandstorm like this, you got indoors. You dropped everything and ran for shelter. People were swept away by these monsters of nature, bundled off by the sandy tide. If you ever knew someone who went missing—and chances are you did—then you'd blame the devils of the sand. "The sands took 'im," people said. And here those devils were again, conspiring with the wind to take the Coilhunter.

He felt himself vanishing into the shifting dust walls. He could barely breathe, even with his mask. If it had been anyone else, with just a neckerchief around their mouth, they would have likely already suffocated. And there'd be no need for a burial, because when the winds settled, the sand would have settled more than six feet overhead.

The monowheel became sluggish. The sand caught in the parts, filling up the exhaust pipes, clogging up the diesel tank. It got everywhere, even in the vents of the Coilhunter's mask. It dug into the wrinkles and crevices of his face, and tried to tunnel under his goggles to finish off his eyes.

The sightlessness and breathlessness brought back flashes of the past, of the blinding fire and smothering smoke. The sting of the sand in the cuts and bruises brought back the burn. Any other time, this would have overwhelmed him, but now it rekindled the fires of wrath in him. He could see nothing ahead, but in his mind's eye, and his mind's crosshairs, he could see Danny Deadmaker and TNT Tom, smiling their crooked smiles.

There was a boom as the monowheel clipped the edge of a hidden mine. He was thrown, and then he felt a sudden drop, and he realised he was tumbling down a dune, with the monowheel somersaulting around him. In the haze of the storm, he didn't know which way was up or down. It must have been a mountain of a dune, for he kept on falling, whacking his arms off the sides of the vehicle, feeling the weight of it drag him up and pull him down, while gravity tried to finish him off.

He struck level ground again, feeling a pang in his left shin as the monowheel came down on him, trapping him. The sands came swiftly, mounting on top of him, shovelling in the first dirt of the grave. He knew he didn't have much time. He had to get free. Despite everything, he had to get shelter.

He hoisted the monowheel up a little and unpinned his leg. Though he had already dug himself out of the sand, it was building around him again. Aaron used to tell him about "a different kind of sand" near the waters, wherever they were, where you could bury yourself up to your neck, or build sand saloons. Little wild Aaron, always dreaming.

Nox got to his feet, feeling one leg sinking into the sand. He pulled it loose and plodded on, yanking one foot free, then the other. The earth kept munching away at him, and he kept on resisting, shielding his face with his gloved hands, not knowing where he was going, only that it had to be away from here.

Then he spotted a bauble of blackness and realised that it was another mine. It was very close, and the wind kept on nudging him towards it. The sun was completely obscured now, but it must've been beaming away, content that finally the land would get him.

But just like TNT Tom, it didn't get him yet.

He trudged on, following the trail of mines, coming out of the storm, watching it sweep behind him like some great tidal wave. The wind died down to a whistle, and Nox pulled off his blocked goggles, halting as he spotted a town on the horizon. He knew where the locals would gather. Any building offered safety, but it was the shelter of the saloon that everyone flocked to, pushed by the stormy winds toward the nearest bottle. Whiskey to lift the spirits. Rum to calm the nerves. Anything to forget your troubles. Yet the Coilhunter didn't come to forget— not this time.

He hobbled on towards the town, spotting the tumbleweeds gathering at the doorways, as if they were just waiting to move in. It was still a trek to go, but normally you'd hear the music from the saloon as the locals made the most of the company. There was nothing like a storm to bring everyone together, to make them see an enemy in the sand instead of each other. But no piano keys carried on that dying wind. No boisterous cries bellowed out through the cracks of the door. No chanting choruses rang out from inebriated lungs. The town looked dead from a distance, which made Nox feel like he, Danny and Tom would be right at home there.

Chapter Thirty-nine

GHOST TOWN

There were a lot of ghost towns in the Wild North, back from the days when it wasn't all desert, when the townsfolk weren't all ghosts. It was always arid there, but it wasn't always sand. The war elsewhere drained the area of good men and women, leaving space for the bad to move in. Some of these tumbleweed towns were now the hideouts for dangerous gangs, but most were too remote for anyone. This looked like one of them.

The Coilhunter strolled up cautiously, dusting off a fallen sign with his foot. Rivertown, it read. He almost scoffed. There were no rivers up here, not now. Everything was old and weathered, but this must've been older than most, maybe older than he felt. If there had been a river nearby, it had long dried up, and the trough was filled in with sand.

He continued on, slowly, through the town, keeping his hands poised at his belt. There were no more mines here, which could have meant anything, but he took it to mean he'd arrived at his destination. This was a shooter's paradise: many windows, more nooks, and much shadow. The eyelid of the sun was almost fully closed now. The red gleam it cast was weak, just enough to give an aura around the buildings, to point out a few—but not all—of the potential places where a rifle might be primed and ready.

Much of the sand had blown out of Rivertown in the storm, leaving behind the cracked earth, with its few straggles of weeds. Somehow they still grew there. Somehow humans did too. He heard the grit break beneath his boots. His ears perked at every noise, his eyes darting to the noisemakers, his hands ready to make some of their own.

He passed a corner shop, Dame Dew's, a confectionery. It brought back memories of his childhood, of hard-boiled sweets and gum drops, and of Old Peggy Coldren, who pushed a cart of home-made sweets through Loggersridge every evening. She was still there decades later, when little Ambrose and Aaron raced out to get their bonbons and lollies. He could almost taste the sweetness, but the memories were sour now.

He continued on, glancing at every window, looking for a shifting shadow, listening for the click of a hammer or trigger. It was deathly silent. Even the wind held its whistles.

He saw the Barons' Bank, all boarded up. That wasn't the property of the Dust Barons, but rather the old royalty and nobility that now went by the name of the Treasury. They were the "government" of old, and even out here in the wild, money ruled. As soon as they acquiesced to the Regime, however, their power quickly waned, and the money-lenders moved in, with their "your cash or your knees" approach. Often they got both.

He continued on to a curve in the street, halting when he heard creaking wood. He turned slowly to see TNT Tom on a rocking chair, looking far too relaxed, looking far too alive.

"You found us," Tom said, puffing on his cigar. "My retirement home."

"Your grave."

Nox swiftly pulled out his pistol, but Tom held up his hand.

"Don't be stupid, Nate."

Nox fought back the urge to pull the trigger. The gun was already cocked and ready.

"You don't want to use gunpowder here," Tom said. He flicked his cigar away. "I already put plenty of that down." The cigar caught something in the sand and set it alight. Nox moved to see what it was, and Tom rocked back completely on his chair, triggering a trap door. He vanished, leaving Nox standing in the middle of a trail of zig-zagging fuses.

Chapter Fourty

BOOBYTRAPS

Nox ran, but he didn't know where he should be running. The entire ground seemed to have been wired, with the wire pressed deep into the cracks. Every building could have been rigged to blow. Many were.

First to go up was the theatre. The fireball sent the roof sky high. The stage was strewn apart, the timber flying out in all directions. Nox raced away from it, feeling the gush of hot air on his tail.

Then the bank blew, just as the Coilhunter passed it. He held his hat on as the blast almost threw him.

Then a line of houses went, one by one, like dominoes. He'd barely got out of the way of one before the next one went up in flames.

By the end of it all, half of Rivertown was flattened or ablaze.

But the Coilhunter was still alive, and so too were TNT Tom and Danny Deadmaker.

Nox strolled through the ruins of the town, ready to run at any moment. Maybe Tom hoped this'd scare him off, but he should've known better. Or maybe Tom wanted him to come, wanted him to press in further, like the spider beckons the fly.

He tried to find the trap door, but it was buried under all the rubble. There must have been another route, so he kept on walking, until he came to an old warehouse. In bygone days, it might have served the workmen on the river. Now it served as one of TNT Tom's hideaways.

He pushed the door open slowly. It was dark inside. He wasn't entirely sure if he should strike a match. He stepped in, then ducked as a blade swung by. He heard Tom's hoarse laugh from up in the rafters.

"Watch your head," he taunted.

Nox took another step, dodging another blade.

"Careful now, Nate."

One more step, and one more blade. This one took a sliver off the brim of his hat.

"Just a little off the top, eh? Snip, snip."

Nox halted. The blades swung back and forth behind him, slicing through the air.

"When're ya gonna stop playin' games?" he rasped.

Tom cackled, then coughed. "Coming from the toymaker." His voice deepened. "You know, you drove me out of business at Loggersridge. It was all well and good when you were just making tidbits for the tots, but then you had to go and move in on mechanics too. That was *my* jurisdiction!"

A steel-tipped log swung down fast. Nox stepped out of the way of it, but he almost stepped into the path of another. He grabbed onto the side of the first log and climbed up it, crouching down, letting it pull him back almost to the still-swinging blades, then send him forward to where he could almost see Tom standing on a platform far above.

"That was just like you, though, Nate, wasn't it?" Tom shouted down. "Stealing my business and stealing my boy's girl. You go riding your high horse around the wilds, saying you're cleaning up the criminals, taking in the thieves, but you were one of them yourself. You didn't mind then, did you?"

Nox said nothing. There was nothing you could say to people like Tom. For some people, once they got an idea in their head, the only way to get it back out again was with a guillotine. Nox wanted to deny the accusations, to say he'd never stolen anything, that he'd worked his trade fair and square, and just did it better than him, and that he'd won Emma's heart fair and square too. If anything, this whole thing just proved she'd made the right choice, even if it did mean her death.

"Got no answer for your crimes, huh?" Tom bellowed. He seemed to be poised and waiting, ready to let loose another trap.

Nox kept perfectly still, vanishing into the shadow as the log pulled him one way, emerging again as it brought him back. He knew the wait would get to Tom. Sometimes the itch got too much and you just had to fire, even though you knew you'd miss the target. Sometimes people were wound up more than the springs in their gun.

Another log came down far to the side, striking nothing but empty air. Of course, Tom had probably worked up a reason to hate that too. When he exhaled, did it steal his breath?

Nox studied the room carefully. There were ladders leading up to the next platform, and more leading higher. All metal. It meant there was no way he could make a leap for them without making some noise. By then, Tom would release the next trap, or run again. Nox wanted this to end, once and for all.

So Nox took his guitar off and hit a button on it, immersing the lower level in smoke. Then he threw the instrument down to the floor, just as he leapt for the nearest ladder. The guitar made a clang, which echoed through the warehouse. Tom set loose another blade, but Nox was already up on the next platform, tip-toeing towards the next ladder.

"Your smoke doesn't scare me, Nate!" Tom shouted.

Nox emerged from the haze behind the man, wrapping his arm around Tom's neck.

"It should."

Chapter Fourty-one

LAST MAN STANDING

Nox dragged TNT Tom out into the streets. The smoke from the burning buildings billowed through in periodic gusts, setting Tom coughing. Nox breathed out black smoke of his own.

"Come out, Danny," he rasped, clicking the hammer of his pistol and pointing it to Tom's head. He kicked the back of Tom's leg, making him fall to his knees.

"He won't come," Tom said.

"Why, 'cause he's a coward?"

"Because he owes you nothing."

"He owes me three lives."

"You'll still be one short if you kill the both of us."

That was true, but two out of three wasn't bad. "Get out here, Danny, or old Tom gets a bullet to the brain."

"And what, you'd let me go free otherwise, Nate?" Tom asked. He hacked up some blood and spit it out.

"Last call, Danny."

Just like the last call at the bar, and the rush that followed, Danny Deadmaker pushed open the saloon doors across the way. He walked out, slow and steady, the spurs on his boots grazing the ground behind him. He kicked them back deliberately, like he always did, drawing a little line in the sand. He didn't do it when he ran from the burning house though. He never left his signature trail then.

He held out his hands. "Well, here I am."

Nox's glare was like gunfire. "At last."

A gust of black smoke blew between them, hiding and revealing them.

"Never thought you'd actually find out," Danny said. "Seems someone blabbed to Waltman. Thought we'd silenced him."

"You thought wrong."

"Let my father go, and we can end this."

"There's only one place he's goin', and you're goin' there too."

Danny glowered at him. He ran his fingers around the brim of his hat. That was another of his signature moves, not long before the draw.

They stared at each other, shooting first with their eyes. The smoke came through again. Danny's hands hovered by his sides, the fingers flexing. One eye squinted. The other widened. The side of his mouth twitched.

He drew, but Nox fired first. Danny clenched his teeth and dropped his gun. The bullet was embedded in his knuckles.

Tom broke free from the Coilhunter's grasp, half-running, half-stumbling towards his son. Nox let him get halfway before he fired a grappling hook towards him. One of the prongs embedded in his shoulder. Nox pulled him back, letting him fall to the ground.

"So this is how it ends," Danny said.

Nox took a step forward. "This is how it ends."

"It won't do you no good, you son of a gun!" Tom roared. He tried to pull the hook free, but Nox let the reflux of the coil drag him back a yard.

"It won't do you any either," Nox said, before firing another bullet. TNT Tom dropped dead right then and there. He'd started the fire, so he probably should've burned. He'd have to burn in Hell instead.

Danny turned on the spot, desperate to run. You could see the fear in his face, even from where the Coilhunter was standing. You didn't need to be a Magi for that.

"You didn't live like one," Nox said, "but you can die like a man."

But Danny ran.

Nox fired at the man's leg, sending him down into the dirt with a cry. Danny tried to crawl away, even as the Coilhunter strolled up next to him.

"Or you can die like the dog you are."

He kicked Danny over onto his back.

"I shoulda killed you too," Danny growled.

"Why didn't ya?"

"I wanted you to suffer. I wanted it to turn you into a shadow of yourself."

"Well, you got what you wanted then. It made me this."

The last round went straight to Danny's skull. Back in the Deadmakers' Den, one of Danny's pals could add another kill to the Coilhunter's tally, and wipe Danny's clean.

Chapter Fourty-two

BURYING THE PAST

The Coilhunter didn't drag the bodies back to the Bounty Booth to cash them in. There were no posters for Danny Deadmaker and TNT Tom, but there was still a big payoff, even if it was just a sense of relief. Nox let the spreading fires of Rivertown cremate them. It seemed fitting.

He found his steel-shielded guitar in the warehouse, though one of the strings was broken. It kind of reminded him of himself. Yet it still put out a mighty tune.

He travelled back to his monowheel, which was half-buried in the sand. The storm was long over now, though maybe it was brewing in another part of the Wild North.

All things considered, the Coilhunter didn't feel as good as he thought he might. The killers were dead, but that didn't bring his family back. Hurting others didn't stop him hurting himself. But it was a start.

He looked up to the sky, where the sun glared back.

"I got 'em, Emma." He sighed. "I got 'em, Ambrose." His sigh was more pained than ever. "I got 'em, Aaron." He shook his head. "Maybe I got 'em too

194

late. Maybe I shoulda been huntin' 'em sooner, before they got to you."

He'd spent countless hours wondering about that, asking himself "what if I did this?" or "what if I did that?" It seemed there was no end of regrets. He'd counted more of them than the bodies he'd buried or dragged back for the reward.

He started up the engine, vowing to continue his mission, to cleanse the Wild North of crime, to stop more killers before they got to someone else. To him, that was the real reward.

Chapter Forty-three

DEBT COLLECTOR

I n a quiet corner of the Burg, a train of carriages pulled up. It was dusk, just after the Dust Barons' curfew, but Blood Johnson obeyed no rules, and no one enforced them against him. He stepped out, flanked by his guards. He had that permanent grin on his face, the one that showed his gold teeth. His hair was gelled back, and his beard was trimmed tight. He had a face of too many victories. The Wild North owed him a defeat.

He swaggered into the safe house, where Handcart Sally was tied up.

"Where's my money?" he asked, never letting the smile fade. It was strange for a smile to show anger. It showed a lot of different emotions on Blood Johnson's face.

"I told you I'd get you it soon."

"Soon is come and gone."

"Please. Just another week."

"You said that last week."

"I got held up. I would've had it. Please, Blood. I can get you it. I just need more time."

"What do you think, Sam?" He turned to the companion at his side, Sam Silver.

"Well, if she's good for it, then she's good for it."

"And if she isn't?"

"Well … then she isn't."

"Words o' wisdom, there," Blood Johnson said to Sally. "How about a trade though? I'll give you another week if you give me one of your fingers. Sure, we can make it a month for a hand."

The glass of the oil lamps shattered and the wicks blew out. The room went black. There was a shuffle of feet as Blood Johnson's men turned wildly. The clamour of their voices betrayed the panic. Sometimes grown men feared the dark.

"Shut your traps, will ya?" Blood Johnson ordered.

Everyone went silent, but their heaving breaths could still be heard, as well as the shaking of guns. Then there was another sound, like the cranking of a lever.

"What was that?" Blood asked. "Who's there?"

Sam Silver perked his ears when he heard a familiar tune, a recognisable strum of a guitar's strings. Others there knew it too, but Blood Johnson only knew it by rumour. That enhanced the sound, added to the fear.

"The Coilhunter," Sam Silver whispered, barely audible. Maybe he was too afraid to draw that awful lawmaker's attention.

"Get us some lights," Blood Johnson barked.

Matches were struck and held out before them.

"What's that?" some of them cried.

In the poor light, they saw what looked like a metal duck standing by the door. A toy. Yet, when the light shone on it, its head moved. It almost seemed to look up at them.

Blood Johnson's jaw dropped. So did the duck's. It quacked.

Then there was a bang like nothing they'd ever heard before, and they felt like their eyes were on fire. Everything turned to a blinding white. The light seemed to invade beyond their sight right into their brains, leaving a searing mark there. The men screamed, dropping their matches and guns, clutching their eyes and dropping to the floor.

Blood Johnson grunted and stumbled about, blinking madly as if the light was like grit in his eyes. The light had long faded in the room, but it wasn't fading fast enough from his sight. He turned around, looking everywhere, as if seeking out some shadows to hide his eyeballs in. Then the light faded a little, enough to see the dark silhouettes of people rolling about on the floor, enough to see the shape of Handcart Sally strapped to the chair, enough to see the formidable outline of the Coilhunter standing next to her, unmoving, like a statue, or like some boogeyman that didn't haunt children, but grown men and women who hadn't let go of their childish ways.

Blood Johnson backed away, falling over the bodies of his men, collapsing to the ground, waving his hands in front of his face, as if swatting away invisible cobwebs. The duck waddled up beside him, and he flinched and cried out when he saw it, though he only saw its outline.

The Coilhunter's silhouette drew in close, leaning

down to him. Now he knew where the stories came from, why so many criminals woke in the black of night, pointing pistols at the shadows of the wall.

"What do you want?" Blood Johnson yelped.

The figure didn't move. It didn't say anything. It let the fear fester, the horror linger.

"Please," Blood Johnson begged. "Let me go. I'll … I'll pay you a fortune."

Still the black shape perched there in the vast whiteness of his blurred and burned vision. Maybe only the rising sun would scare away the shadow. He knew too well that the night had only started, that the nightmare had just begun.

"I've come," the Coilhunter rasped, "to pay a debt." How many horrors had spoken with that voice in the restless sleep of the wrong? How many had heard that grit, like the voice of the desert itself, seeking retribution?

The Coilhunter's gloved hand came in, holding something. Blood Johnson clenched every muscle in his body involuntarily. That something could've been anything. Knowing the rumours, it might even have been a clockwork butterfly.

It wasn't.

He felt the cold metal, the round edges.

It was a bullet.

"The debt was in iron," the Coilhunter croaked, "but I'm payin' it in lead."

Blood Johnson trembled.

"Well," the Coilhunter said, "scram."

Blood Johnson rolled onto his belly and wormed away. The bullet rolled to the ground and spun there for a moment.

"Wait," Nox said.

Blood Johnson froze.

"Don't forget your payment."

The ganglord shimmied over on his elbows, feeling around on the ground for the little nugget of lead. He scurried away on his hands and knees, out the front door into the safety of the night, where his men had already vanished. All the while as he fled, he tried not to look back, not to that towering shadow, not to the gunslinger, the lawmaker, the Coilhunter.

WHAT'LL YOU DO?

"Thanks," Handcart Sally said.

She rubbed her reddened wrists as the bonds were cut, then pulled down the blackened goggles the Coilhunter had placed over her eyes before the light blast. He was still wearing his. He almost didn't look human with those and the mask on. Maybe that was the point. Maybe they weren't just practical.

"Told ya you didn't need to worry."

"Well," she said. "You were cuttin' it pretty close there."

He smirked. "Better to let them think they're almost gettin' away with it, then make 'em realise they never truly can."

"You let him go though."

"Did I?"

"Sure looked like it."

"But now he's in a prison of the mind. He's had a hauntin'. He'll spread the word, make others like him afraid. When a big man trembles, all the little men take heed."

"I hope you're right."

"I'm just using their weapon against 'em. Fear."

"What about your own mission? Did you get 'em?"

"I got 'em good."

He turned to leave, but she grabbed his arm.

"Wait," she said. "Why don't you ... stay?"

"I can't."

"Why not?"

"I'm just a wanderer." He thought of little Aaron, wild wanderer.

"You don't have to be alone, y'know."

He sighed. "I do."

"It seems to me you're not just punishing criminals. You're punishing yourself."

"Well, there ain't no saints out here."

"We ain't all sinners either."

"Oh, we are, in one way or another. I think we have to be to live here."

"Now that you've completed your mission," Sally said, "what'll you do?"

"Oh, I've only completed part of it."

"The nasty part?"

The Coilhunter smiled beneath his mask. "There's some nasty parts to come. Ya see, this here world's got a disease."

"And you're the cure?"

"No," Nox said, pulling out a pistol and cocking the trigger. "This is."

"You can't put them all out to pasture."

"There ain't no pastures to put 'em in. But there's ground. Plenty o' that."

"It won't fulfil you, y'know."

"It doesn't have to."

"It won't make you happy."

"Maybe not, but it'll make some people happy. It'll save some lives. It'll make this world a safer place."

Sally smiled. "With you in it?"

"For the good people, yeah. For the conmen and the criminals, there ain't no such thing as 'safe' any more. Doesn't matter where they hide, or for how long. I'm comin' for 'em. Sooner or later. Sure as that damn sun rises, as there's dust in the desert." He paused. "What'll *you* do? Now that you're free."

She rubbed her wrists again. "I dunno. Could do burial work for bounty hunters."

He said nothing, but his eyes said it all.

"Sorry." She paused. "I guess there's always the Ruby District."

"You ain't workin' there."

"What, you care?"

"There's one too many o' the Hays sisters turnin' tricks already."

"It's a fallback."

"It's another prison."

"A prison that pays."

"You can aim higher than that."

She grabbed the buckle of her belt with both hands. "I guess I always wanted to look after horses."

Nox raised an eyebrow. "Horsetamer Sally."

"A girl can dream."

"A girl can do anything she wants." He turned, halted, then looked back. "Just … you know, keep off those Wanted posters."

He walked off into the sunset, into that glaring red globe, as if he was coming for it too. His silhouette stood out starkly against the red aura, a black, intimidating shape. It was the same shape the criminals had grown to dread, that many saw in their nightmares, and many more saw in the terrors of the day.

ABOUT THE AUTHOR

Dean F. Wilson was born in Dublin, Ireland in 1987. He started writing at age 11, when he began his first (unpublished) novel, entitled *The Power Source*. He won a TAP Educational Award from Trinity College Dublin for an early draft of *The Call of Agon* (then called *Protos Mythos*) in 2001.

He is the author of the *Children of Telm* epic fantasy trilogy, the *Great Iron War* steampunk series, the *Coilhunter Chronicles* science-fiction western series, and the *Hibernian Hollows* urban fantasy series.

Dean also works as a journalist, primarily in the field of technology. He has written for *TechEye*, *Thinq*, *V3*, *VR-Zone*, *ITProPortal*, *TechRadar Pro*, and *The Inquirer*.

www.deanfwilson.com

Made in the USA
Middletown, DE
24 July 2021